GATHERING DARKNESS

CHRIS ALLINOTTE

This book is dedicated to Aimee, William and Matthew, who give me all the light I need to write about the dark.

VELOX BOOKS
Published by arrangement with the author.

Gathering Darkness copyright © 2022
by Chris Allinotte.

All Rights Reserved.

This book is a work of fiction. People, places, events, and situations are the product of the author's imagination. Any resemblance to actual persons, living or dead, or historical events, is purely coincidental.

No part of this book may be reproduced, stored in a retrieval system, or transmitted by any means without the written permission of the author and publisher.

CONTENTS

Coming Home — 1

Sex and Beer — 12

Scratch — 18

Bones of Contention — 19

The Doll Maker and the Rat — 23

Devil's Night — 28

Pick Your Own Pumpkin — 46

Newspaper Hat — 50

Kittens for Sale — 51

The Moustache — 54

The Sins of the Past — 66

The Choir of Pulcinello — 73

Game Night — 75

Adaptation — 89

Tempting Morsels — 91

Turn Around	93
Fear Combined	96
Mopping Up	106
A Fairy Tale	109
Treasures of the Deep	110
Freedom Within Reach	113
The Cabin Sleeps	115
Fun in the Sun	121
Something Different	125
Frosted Glass	128
Postage Due, Pandora	131
Eat Me	142
On-y Dancer	143
Story Notes	146
Acknowledgements	151
About the Author	152

COMING HOME

Ty woke with a jolt. For one terrible moment, he could still feel the oily barrel of Lenny Dallas' automatic pressed to his forehead. He rubbed at the spot, and his breathing started to slow as he looked out into the hallway through the open bedroom door. Everything was silent and, with no electricity, the only light came from the failing streetlight outside, and the cell phone on the nightstand reading four-thirty. Beside him, Shauna still slept peacefully, lost in the strange, Percocet-flavoured world she would doubtless tell him all about in the morning. Ty looked at her sagging green panties, and the way she'd tangled herself up with the sheets and felt an urge to gather her to him, both to protect her and take comfort in her warmth.

Protect her? Like you 'protected' Regan? He frowned at the unwelcome thought and then dismissed it. Regan was a long time ago. Shauna was who he was with now. She was who he had to worry about.

With one finger, he touched the calf that was sticking out from a tangle of sheets, and lightly followed the outline of Bettie Page that was tattooed there. When they first met, he used to trace the delicate, vibrant tattoos that covered her body with his tongue. He loved following their curves, and the sensual thrill that Shauna had taken from it.

Now, as her skin had paled and taken on the waxy hue of serious addiction, the designs looked tired and poor Bettie, whose inky lips he'd tasted in moments of passion, looked depressed. He brought his hand to rest on her ass, and left it there, feeling her breathe. The warmth of her at least was comforting in the dark. She gave a loud snore and shifted under the sheets. He smirked. The pills didn't have that printed in their list of side effects—"Caution, may cause loss of sensuality, as you'll sound like a rusty chainsaw when you sleep."

Suddenly, Ty wanted to shove Shauna hard, to roll her off the bed, to shock her. He took his hand away, took a breath, and counted to ten in his head. There was a big reckoning coming over Shauna's drug use, but four in the morning was not the time to do it—especially when there were bigger pressures closing in around the two of them. *And it's not all her fault, you asshole.* There was truth in that as well.

He gave Shauna's ass a gentle squeeze, then turned over and went back to sleep.

✳✳✳

Bang. Bang. Bang.

Ty pulled the sheets up and tried to ignore the sound. It was probably something going on outside, anyway. At least, he tried to convince himself of that. His sleep had been dreamless and restful for once, and he wasn't about to let it go easily.

Bang. Bang. Bang.

Except that it was coming from inside the house. He got up and padded into the hall, rubbing his eyes with the heel of his hand. Looking over the railing to the dark foyer below, Ty listened for the sound to come again. If he was lucky, it would be the cops. They might get turned out for squatting, probably fined, too—though he was sure they'd left no trace of their entry. If it wasn't the cops though...

Christ, what are we doing here? He was fully awake now and cursing himself for thinking they'd found a temporary respite from their problems.

If being on the run had taught Ty anything, it was that he was reckless—not fearless, not stoic—reckless. Reckless people did stupid things. Being reckless was what led him from a bad position selling dope to a worse position owing for dope. And that led to the position he was in right now—where being busted by the cops for trespassing was the least of his worries.

He crept down the stairs, holding the railing. If he tripped in the dark and broke something, he'd be as good as dead. Going to an Emergency Room would be the same as putting an ad on TV advertising their location.

As the oak bannister slid beneath his hand, his thoughts drifted back to his brief but happy time with Regan here. They had fixed this staircase together. That had been one of the best weekends and had ended with the two of them covered in sawdust, drinking beer on the bottom step, and later making earnest, exhausted love on the living room floor. Four months later, everything had gone to shit.

(you're hurting me)

When the banks collapsed in 2007, Ty's occasional drug use had developed into a full-time career, but the money he made selling the stuff was nowhere near enough to get out from under two crippling mortgages. It wasn't even enough to pay down a maxed out line of credit and six different credit cards. He'd had to walk away from the house he and Regan had considered their "forever home."

(please Ty. Please.)

Losing the house had been like pulling the plug in a boat. Everything started going down. Within weeks of the default, Regan was gone too. He burned friends and family on short term loans that went straight up his nose. Soon, everything that Ty had been working for—everything he'd been—was completely gone.

What happened next was completely unexpected. With nothing left to lose, he had nothing left to prove. It was as if he'd been bound in a straitjacket that he couldn't feel, only to be released from it one day and realize then that he'd been trapped. Being nothing was by far more intoxicating than anything he'd ever peddled out of his car.

The only person he owed anything to now was himself... and Leonard Dallas, of course. He'd sold the last of his coke and kept all the cash—including Dallas' cut. Leonard Dallas, Ty knew, would give less than a shit about his new outlook on life.

(hurting me)

Ty left town. He'd never talked about his past in front of the boss. Dallas knew he was from "Back East", and nothing else. The gangster would eventually track him down but staying where the risk of getting busted was sky-high made the plan just crazy enough to work—for a little while, at least.

Bang. Bang. Bang.

Or had it? Were Dallas's men just outside? Maybe Dallas had sent Gerard after him—that skinny psycho scared Ty almost as much as Dallas did.

Bang. Bang. Bang. Bang.

Ty stared at the door. It hadn't moved. The padlock was holding firm, and the sound wasn't coming from the jimmied door at the back of the house, either.

He was scanning the living room, which was barely visible in the light that filtered through the boards on the window. A thought occurred to him. He ran back upstairs to the bedroom and looked inside. The bed was empty and a pale blue glow was coming from the ensuite toilet. Shauna must be in there. She was forever running down her battery, using the cell phone as a flashlight. He'd told her over and over that there was no way to charge the thing in the house. Still, the noise had unnerved him a little, and he was glad to find her awake.

"Shauna?" he called. There was no answer. He walked into the room. "Babe? You there? You hearing this noise?"

Nothing.

Ty went to the bathroom door. The phone was in there, Shauna wasn't.

Bang... Bang... Bang.

Still holding the phone, he ran back downstairs, forgetting his caution as annoyance turned to worry. If she was sleepwalking again...

He reached the kitchen and stopped. The silence had coalesced into a dull and viscous hum. A car went by outside, and Ty jumped.

Shauna wasn't down here, either. His mind was churning. Normally, the Oxy made her sleep straight through the night, but once or twice before she'd gone sleepwalking. There had been a brutal time a while back in Lubbock, Texas. They were holed up in a sixty-dollar motel room with a coin slot on the bed and grease stains on the wall. Their second night, Ty had woken to find the door open and Shauna gone. When he'd finally found her, she was naked, and wading ever deeper into the algae–choked muck that used to be a swimming pool. He'd shaken her roughly awake, and she'd freaked out—screaming and clawing at him with her ragged junkie nails. It had taken an hour to get her to calm down and longer to get her back to bed.

Ty hoped this wasn't another episode like that. Right now, though, he just wanted to find her.

The banging came again, and his breath caught at the back of his throat. It was coming from the basement.

His heart, already racing, began pounding in his ears. Now that he could hear the sound more clearly, he had a bitter, gnawing sensation that he'd heard the same noise before, and that he should recognize it.

He opened the basement door and paused for a second. The streetlights coming through the boards on this level made it possible to see what was in front of him; in the cellar, it would be pitch black. What the hell was she doing down there? He realized at that moment that he was still holding Shauna's phone. With a tap of the screen, the phone lit up and he could see the top two stairs directly in front of him. At the very least, he wouldn't break his neck before he found out what was going on.

The steps creaked as he started down. That noise mixed with a fresh round of banging, and the final pieces of the memory he'd been chasing clicked together. Regan.

It couldn't be...

(...you're hurting me...)

As if conjured by the thought of her name, Ty's last night in this house began to play out again, as it had in his nightmares ever since.

***

He was high. He was always high now. It was the only thing that made sense to him and the only thing, Regan included, that gave him any relief from the increasing pile of shit he was facing. Where was it? Ty kicked aside the two moving boxes he'd already torn apart into the darkest corner of the basement. Halfway through a third, he finally found the jewellery box. The tiny oak and ebony chest had sat on their dresser in the old house. Here, they were still finishing the renovations before they got the rest of the unpacking done. There was a tiny pewter key; thankfully, it hadn't fallen out. Ty turned the key and there, on top, was Great Granny's diamond necklace. He lifted it out.

"What are you doing?"

He jumped. When he turned, he saw Regan wearing the sad little frown that dominated her expressions so much these days.

"I'm selling these." Fuck it, he thought, no need to deny it now.

"They're not yours to sell." There wasn't the slightest bit of warmth in her voice. "You make me sick, Ty. Put those down."

"And what do you suppose we'll do for money then, Regan, huh?" he yelled. His temper, never far away when he was high, raged now. Regan, to his surprise and increasing anger, didn't back down.

"Maybe, Ty, if you sold more of that shit than you put up your nose, we wouldn't be in this position. Put those down now." She yelled the last, matching his intensity. He'd been in the process of slipping the necklace into his pocket, now he flung it at her. She flinched, and he lashed out with a fist, catching her high in the chest.

Something snapped then. He wasn't even seeing Regan anymore. His body had tasted what it was to hurt something, and it liked it. All the injustice, all the impotence he'd felt, came rushing out of him, and he threw punch after punch. Regan stumbled back. Her head hit the water tank with a dull thud.

"Please…" she said through sobs, "Please Ty, you're… you're hurting me."

It was such an absurd thing to say that it caused him to pause for a moment. But it was too late, the mixture of drugs and adrenaline had whipped him into a frenzy that couldn't be stopped now. He screamed and threw himself forward.

The cellar reverberated with the sound of bone meeting metal.
Bang. Bang. Bang.

***

He shook his head. Over. Everything was over. Regan was over.

The stairs groaned as they took his weight. Cracked linoleum bit at his bare feet as he walked down.

The flashlight picked out a hard white circle that shone on random details: a steel pillar, the gaping hole of a lidless drain, his old workbench. The sound was louder now, coming from the far corner, where the water heater stood.

Ty took a deep breath. His sense of dread was nearly paralyzing, but he forced himself forward. A moment later, the light picked out a naked thigh, with a faded tattoo of Bettie Page winking back at him.

Shauna was facing the corner, wearing only the sagging, green panties she'd been sleeping in. Again and again, she slammed her forehead into the side of the hot water tank. There was a large bloody smear at the point of contact. He came around to the side and shone the light at her face. Shauna's eyes were rolled up to the whites. Her jaw hung slack. Ty felt sick. It wasn't as if she was about to knock herself unconscious—she was already unconscious. There was a terrible impression of concavity to her brow, but it was hard to make out anything in the mass of swelling, bruises, and flowing blood that had replaced his lover's face. She reared back to butt the heater again.

"Stop!" he shouted, putting a hand out to catch her forehead as it swung. She kept going and mashed his hand back against the metal.

He cried out, then grabbed Shauna by the shoulders and shook her.

"Wake up! For God's sake, wake up!"

Shauna's eyes flew open, and she screamed. It was a feral, primal sound. Her hand came up into the light, holding the adjustable chrome wrench from his tool bench. The thing was the size of a baseball bat and had been his best friend when he used to screw around fixing his car. He hadn't been able to find it before the move and had regretted leaving it behind. Now, here it was again—swinging two handed in a heavy arc towards his face. Ty threw up a hand and caught Shauna's wrists. She was shaking with the effort to hit him and screaming, still screaming. The wrench was wobbling back and forth.

"Shauna! Babe! It's me!" he screamed.

She pulled free, swung hard, and connected with his jaw.

The basement went darker.

***

Ty woke up.

His jaw was throbbing in time with his pulse. He touched his face and withdrew his fingers with a wince. The flesh there felt spongy and hot. The phone's screen was still glowing beside him, but was now starting to grow dim. He stood up and staggered back to the stairs. He could see bloody footprints stamped on the linoleum all the way up. Shauna. What the fuck?

Upstairs, the front door was open. Pieces began to come together in his mind. It was the drugs, had to be. Something inside Shauna's head had finally gone bad. At some point during her episode, she must have crossed the final border between sleepwalking and psychosis. There was no sign of her having gone outside. How far could she have gone with her face in such a disastrous state? It was a wonder she had still been on her feet when he'd found her—let alone strong enough to attack him. So where was she?

He stepped outside on to the cold interlocking brick walkway. The street was empty, but he felt horribly exposed. There was no blood out here. His brain, so recently rattled, was trying to catch up to the moment and reason out what he was seeing. If Shauna was still in the grip of her nightmares, she couldn't have reasoned well enough to go upstairs, get the padlock key from his pocket, and return downstairs with it to open the hasp and leave. If she'd woken up, she'd almost certainly be lying somewhere, screaming in pain with what she'd done to herself. So, if Shauna hadn't opened the door... Dallas. It had to be Dallas' men.

Ty went back into the house and sprinted up the stairs two at a time. He stopped dead in front of the bedroom door. There was blood on the floor. Every part of him wanted to flee, to get in his car and drive until everything started to make sense again. But he wouldn't get far in just his boxers. He had a clear mental picture of his key ring sitting in its usual place in the right front pocket of his jeans. With luck, his wallet would be in the back pocket, and he could just grab the pants and get out of here. His heart was pounding. In the muted light from the window, he saw that his pants were crumpled by the side of the bed near the bathroom floor. Without another thought, he ran into the room, intent on grabbing the jeans.

The silence of the room was split with a bowel chilling scream of rage from behind him. He whipped his head around to see Shauna staggering out of the bathroom. Blood had poured over her skin, coating her breasts, belly, and panties. Her face was like rotten liver, and her mouth gaped open in its moment of feral triumph. He put an arm up to defend himself as she swung the wrench again. Pain like liquid lightning shot through his arm as the bones shattered. The blow had enough momentum that the head of the wrench still connected with the top of his head, leaving him dazed. He sat down hard. His own blood started flowing, running into his eyes. With his uninjured hand he tried to clear it and realized there were bright spots blooming there as well. He was going to pass out. If he did, he'd die. Shauna reared back for another attempt.

"Enough." It was another woman's voice. In his semi–conscious state, Ty couldn't recognize the speaker, but whoever it was had attracted Shauna's wrath away from him. She screamed again. Ty passed out to the sound of the wrench hitting bone.

Bang. Bang. Bang.

When Ty came to, he was lying in bed. His injured arm, now swollen to the size of a roast of beef, lay on his stomach. His jaw was throbbing, and his head felt worse. The pillow felt sticky against his cheek.

Shauna, where was Shauna? He turned his head, wincing and fighting through waves of pain. There, beside the bed, was the mangled ruin that had been his girlfriend. Mercifully, she was face down in a puddle of her own blood and hair.

Something touched his injured arm, and he screamed.

"Welcome home, lover." The voice was the second woman he'd heard before everything went black. There was a low chuckle, and then, "She seemed nice."

As Ty rolled over, he knew what he was going to see, though his whole being screamed against it. Regan was lying next to him, a cold white hand on his arm. She was naked. Even her face was unblemished. Outside of all rational thought, his body began to respond to her touch. She brought her other hand to rest on his chest. It was still holding the bloody wrench.

"How?" was what he wanted to say. Nothing came out. Regan seemed to understand anyway.

"You left me here, Ty," she said. "Left me in our dream house. Our house."

He worked his lips, trying to form sounds . Nothing was working. Regan laid a finger on his lips. "It was our forever home. Remember?"

Ty nodded.

"Well darling," she cooed, still using the same calm, almost sensual tone, "I came back to look for you when we got separated. And when you didn't come—I decided to wait."

Ty's voice broke loose of his trembling lips, "I… I… ki…"

"You broke my heart," said Regan. "But now you're back, and we can be happy again. Forever."

"Sh–Shauna…"

Regan smiled. It was a smile he'd seen countless times before, when she'd pointed out something that should be blatantly obvious to him. He'd always thought of it as her "Oh, you silly boy" smile.

"I told you I've been waiting, Ty. I've only had our house to talk to. And after awhile, it listened." She smiled again. "Not long after that, it started talking back." Regan touched the end of his nose. He stifled a scream.

"It didn't like being left alone either," she said, stroking the wall. "We're friends now."

With a sudden flicker of movement, like the stutter of a television signal, Regan was suddenly standing next to Shauna's body.

"Your friend heard us talking, I think." Regan shoved the corpse with her foot. Shauna's body was limp and moved away from the ground with a horrible squelching sound.

Looking back at him, Regan said, "I don't think she was all that stable, Ty." She took her foot away and Shauna's body fell back against the sodden carpet with an almost soundless thump.

"I found her in the basement. This place is full of memories, and she got kind of trapped down there—though what she could have been seeing, I couldn't say."

A flicker. Regan was back in bed with him. "Do you have any idea what she saw?"

Ty shook his head.

"Hmm…" she sighed. "Whatever it was, I think it broke her mind." She smiled and looked Ty in the eye. Her irises had become so pale blue they were almost white. "Lucky for you, I stopped her before she broke yours."

Suddenly, Ty was aware of footsteps downstairs. There were at least two people walking around on the hardwood.

"…check it out and call in."

"What if he's here?"

"Kill him, and call in. Gerard said to call either way."

Ty tried to sit up. Regan pushed him back. Her hands were like ice coated in silk.

"Where are you going, Ty?" she asked.

He was frantic. There was no time to waste. But what could he do?

Regan frowned. "Don't leave me again, Ty. Don't."

The steps grew louder. They were coming up the stairs. Regan seemed to notice.

"I see. Your friends are here."

"Yeah," cried Ty, trying to keep his voice as low as possible. "They're going to kill me Regan."

She smiled. "That's wonderful, Ty."

He stopped moving. "What?"

"They'll have guns, right?"

He nodded.

"Then someone will hear, and eventually, they'll come take the bodies away." Leaning in, she kissed him on the mouth with hard, implacable lips. She seemed to be sucking the breath out of him.

When she broke the kiss, she whispered in his ear, "Then it can just be you and me again, in our forever home."

"I hear something up here." The voice came from the top of the steps.

Tears started rolling down Ty's cheeks. He looked at Regan and whispered, "I don't want to die."

Regan's body flickered once more, and she was straddling him. "In the bedroom! Let's go."

"Make love to me, Ty."

"I…I…" *can't* he wanted to say. His body said otherwise. She flickered, and they were together.

"Be with me, Ty," she moaned, moving her hips. "Let go of your fear."

Metal on metal clicking. A bullet being chambered.

"Love me Ty. Love me now."

Ty closed his eyes and reached out to his wife. She clasped her fingers around his.

Bang.

SEX AND BEER

The brewery had been closed so long it no longer smelled of sour beer. Joey liked the organic, slightly yeasty odour that remained. Sam clung to his waist, huddling against the chill that found its way through scores of broken windows. Their footfalls echoed among the bare girders and abandoned vats.

"Over here, let's go," said Sam, pulling away and tugging him by the hand. She led Joey down a narrow corridor. He liked her aggressiveness; it was one of the things that had convinced him to leave the bar with her. The aggressive chicks were usually animals in bed.

"I worked here one summer, about five years ago," she said. Joey hadn't asked, but if she wanted to talk, it was no skin off his ass. Speaking of asses, he was relishing the view as she led the way. He wondered if she was drunk enough for that. A thrill ran up his spine and he shuddered a little. This was shaping up to be an epic night.

"This was my boss' office," she continued, as they passed an otherwise ordinary looking door. Sam's tone had cooled and carried an edge that hadn't been there before. Joey didn't push. Something had obviously happened; she didn't want to talk about it. Fine. The last thing he wanted to do was spoil the mood. The large pane of dusty glass had a spiderweb of cracks around a large jagged hole in the centre. On the ground were shards of glass and the remains of a broken bottle. Someone got bad news, he thought, and chuckled a little.

"What did you say?" she asked.

Joey hadn't said a word. Before he could answer, she continued, "Nothing. Never mind. Later."

She wasn't talking to him.

All right, he thought, that's a little crazy.

Sam took off her jean jacket, exposing her naked back. The skin was creamy-smooth and perfect below the thin black neck of her halter top. Joey smiled. What did it matter if she was a little "off?" Look at her, he thought. She had no idea of the things he wanted to do to her, the things he was going to do to her. He tried to remember if he'd brought a rubber. He was supposed to wear one now. Every time, the doctors said. If not though, he wasn't going to worry about it. He got along fine. She'd be fine too.

It was uncomfortably dry in the office, and the smell of long dead yeast and hops was making Joey want a beer in the worst way, though he'd had several at the bar already. His tongue felt like sandpaper in his mouth. *After*, he thought. Yeah. *After we* fuck. Thinking the word excited him. They were going to break into the shitty, dusty little office of this old brewery, and *fuck*. He tugged at the leg of his jeans, which were getting tighter.

Joey tried to calm down . It wasn't cool to look too eager. He thought of the beer again. That would be the best damned beer of his life. Sam was easily the hottest girl he'd ever seen—there was no way she was getting away.

"What's in here?" he asked, moving to a plain grey metal door set in the back wall.

"This is what I wanted to show you," said Sam. He saw that her smile had returned. She was meeting his gaze with her own large black eyes. In the darkness, they were so wide the whites were almost gone. The naked hunger he saw there was more than enough to rekindle his excitement. She turned the knob and revealed a room not much bigger than a closet. There was a small cot in the corner with a yellowing, tattered sheet stretched across it. He checked his pockets again. No dome. It was no big deal. He'd pull it out and pop on that perfect back of hers, or something. Another shiver rippled through him. *What's with me?* he thought. You'd think this was my first time, or something.

"Shall we?" asked Sam.

"Yeah," Joey agreed. He stepped forward to push her into the room and was surprised when she grabbed him instead.

"Wonderful," she said, and threw him roughly to the bed. Her manic energy was what had set her apart from the other bar rats and trailer trash. Now that same energy was getting him so worked up, he began to worry about not being able to last. Sam spread her legs and dropped heavily onto his bulging jeans. Her coal coloured hair draped in front of her face. Without brushing it aside, she leaned in and began kissing his neck.

Joey moaned. Sam ran her hands under his shirt and scoured his chest and stomach with her nails. She yanked down on his pants, and then she was riding him. Her body was a taut, dancing live wire. His hips bucked. He was way too close but couldn't think of what to say or what to do. She was all over him, so absorbed in the moment that she'd given up all pretence of delicacy. Her lips smacked as she kissed him harder and longer.

"Not yet," she moaned.

"All right… all right," he grunted in return, willing himself to keep control.

"Soon," said Sam. Her voice was distant again, and he had that same feeling, that she wasn't talking to him. It was weird, all right. At the same time, the distraction was helping fight off the point of no return. He took the game to her and scoured her back with his nails. She threw her head back and laughed. Joey threw his back and moaned.

Suddenly, Sam pulled back, and sat on his thighs. She was staring him in the eye. If her attention had ever wandered, it was all the way back now. Her black eyes gleamed behind the obsidian curtain of her hair. The sudden withdrawal of her attention made Joey's body cry out. Everything was tingling and throbbing.

"Are you having a good time, Joey?"

He tried to speak but could only gasp for air. He nodded.

"That's good, Joey," she moaned. "My turn now, 'kay?"

He nodded again.

Sam leaned in again, and this time, instead of kissing, she opened her mouth impossibly wide and bit deeply into his neck at the shoulder. Joey tried to scream. She clamped a hand like a hydraulic press across his windpipe, and only a gurgling wheeze came out. The other hand that had been exploring and teasing the hairs on his stomach grew hard and dug deeply into the flesh there. There was an awful feeling of being *entered*. The world started to swim in front of his eyes and he welcomed the coming blackness. He remained aware long enough, though, to see four triple-jointed legs erupt from the back of his would-be lover. The hairy black appendages stretched and flexed in the air. Her skin peeled away in thick bloody strips to reveal a bulging black abdomen with the clear bloody imprint of an hourglass in the centre.

The Samantha-thing lowered thick black mandibles to his gushing shoulder. An all-too-human tongue ran out between them and lapped at the blood. Underneath the monstrous castanet clicking of the spider, Joey could still hear the girl he'd met a million years ago at the bar. Incredibly, she sounded pissed off.

"Stupid, stupid, stupid! How are we going to get anywhere if you won't let us mate first?" The mandibles seemed to click in reply, holding up their end of this obscene conversation.

"Yes, I suppose," said Sam's distant voice, "Better luck next time, then."

Mercifully, he didn't see what happened next. Spots bloomed in front of his eyes. As he slipped away, he thought he heard screaming. The swirling colours widened briefly to a grey test pattern, and finally everything went black.

***

Joey woke up. That in itself was a surprise. His shoulder, which had been spouting a generous helping of his blood, had become a churned, purple clot beside his neck. He couldn't feel it, he couldn't feel *anything* in his extremities. On the other hand, his insides felt like they were burning up. His stomach was roiling, and he felt vicious cramps throughout his chest and bowels.

Also, he seemed to be dangling.

Long ropy strands of white web radiated out from him in every direction. The same stuff bound him in a loose cocoon. He followed one sticky cable to the curved edge of the wall. The sick-sour tang of beer, absent in the building, was overpowering in here.

From the darkness somewhere below, he heard Samantha's voice.

"What did you do to us?" The spider's clicking was gone, and only the voice of a sincerely pissed off woman remained.

At the limit of his vision, two obsidian legs appeared from the shadows. As the shape climbed higher, Joey began to scream. Samantha had partially re–emerged from the body of the spider. The torso and head were the same woman he'd been drinking with just hours ago, but her arms and legs were those of the spider. She scaled the wall until she was level with Joey and then turned to face him.

She was naked, and despite the multiple horrors of the situation, he still had a faint thrill at the sight of her. Something was wrong with her, though. An ugly deep yellow stain was spreading across her chest.

"What did you do?" she repeated. Her voice was almost a scream, and her lips were pulled back from teeth that now tapered to gleaming points.

Joey was breathing hard. The pain in his guts and his brain's attempts to reject what he was seeing had kept him from answering immediately. He took a good look at her. The spider's second and third legs were starting to curl in towards Sam's body. They were twitching. While he watched, the deep yellow patch on her ribs deepened and spread. Something clicked for him. He knew what was going on.

She started to shout at him again, but he didn't listen.

He was laughing. It felt awful, like he was about to shit out his insides. Still, there was nothing for it. She'd done something to him already . He was going to die. But the thing that made her so powerful, made her overly vulnerable to his own special problem. He was glad that he hadn't worn a rubber now. That made him laugh harder, and now he tasted blood.

"Stop laughing!" she screamed. "You, your blood…"

"It's… it's just the Hep, babe," said Joey. Knowing she was dying too had driven the terror from him. "Hep B, to be exact." He laughed again. "Ah. Shit. That hurts. You… you should go see a doctor. He'll clear you right up."

With a primal shriek, Sam lunged forward on her remaining legs, and drove her topmost legs through his chest. It hurt like nothing he'd ever felt before, and the sensation of the legs as alive within him was somehow even worse.

Samantha's face was now right in front of his own. Surprisingly, her tone had dropped to normal, but the spider's clicks were very noticeable behind her words.

"You *bastard*," she said. "You were going to have sex with me and leave me infected?"

He looked her squarely in the eyes. "Pretty much, yeah." He smiled. "It's not actually that bad for me. But I understand if you don't do anything about it, it can get pretty serious."

The spider-woman gritted her teeth together and drew back. In a single fluid motion, she ripped his body wide open as the legs jerked free. The cocoon fell free from the web, and Joey tumbled to the floor of the vat. There, he found himself atop a pile of similar spun shells, dozens of desiccated corpses, and the stinking reek of sour beer.

As his consciousness retreated for the last time, he watched the spider-woman high above twitch in her own death throes . He wished once more for a final brew. He was just so damned *thirsty*.

SCRATCH

Monday morning, there was an unpleasant itching in my forearm. I thought I'd slept on it. By afternoon, it had settled in to become a deep electrical thrum of discomfort.

... slowly now, careful, drag with the flat of the razorblade...

Tuesday morning, it felt as if a colony of termites were setting up house near my elbow. The skin was corrugated and raw from ploughing with my fingernails.

... there it is... a tender spider–web... it is the shape of agony...

Wednesday, I bled a lot.

... lapping up red copper to clear the view... I bend tooth to nerve...

I'll eat myself well.

BONES OF CONTENTION

"Where are all the skeletons?"

"What? What are you talking about?" asked Taylor, lowering his book. He stared at Jonathan. This was going to be something stupid. He just *knew* it.

Jonathan put down the binoculars, "You know, *skeletons*. Like, bones... of people?"

Taylor threw a sneaker at him. It bounced off the heavy glass of the open balcony door.

"Why'd you do that?" asked Jonathan, sounding genuinely surprised.

"I know what skeletons are, you asshole," said Taylor, leaning back into the sofa.

"Well then," continued Jonathan, "What do you think? They're undead too, aren't they?"

"They can't *move*, Jon. There's nothing attached to their bones—no muscles, *nothing*."

Now Jonathan was the one that looked annoyed. He started pacing the apartment—this didn't take long. Their "bachelor pad" was just fifteen feet on a side. Jon would walk five steps to the wall, turn, and walk five steps back—it drove Taylor crazy. He looked like a cardboard duck in a shooting gallery. Taylor squeezed his eyes shut; this was going to be a long evening.

"Look," started Jonathan, "you're telling me the dead have come back to life—for which there is no good scientific reason—leaving only the supernatural, but I'm supposed to believe skeletons are somehow exempt from this... what... magic?"

Taylor tossed his book aside. This was idiotic, and he opened his mouth to say so, but Jonathan held up a hand.

"Wait a minute."

Jon had stopped at the balcony door again and resumed looking through the binoculars. Now he swapped the field glasses for the hunting rifle in the corner. He slipped on the orange ear protectors that were clipped to the barrel and stepped outside.

"Firing."

Pissed off or not, Taylor knew not to mess around. He jammed his fingers into his ears. The report was deafening in their tiny apartment.

Jonathan put the gun down. Taylor cocked a questioning eyebrow. Instead of answering, Jon came back in, put down the gun, and walked to the little white message board near the kitchen. He drew a single stroke with the marker under today's date. They were ahead of yesterday by three already.

"Now," said Jonathan, "back to the skeletons."

Taylor's head was still reeling from the report of the shot, but Jon's dogged worrying about this stupid topic couldn't go on. Taking a deep breath, Taylor asked, "Jon, how do you kill a zombie?"

"You shoot it in the head."

"And why?"

"To destroy its brain," answered Jon, with a tone that said, *obviously*.

"Exactly," shouted Taylor. "There can't be walking skeletons, because they've got no brains, and if you keep on beating this thing to death, they're not alone."

Jonathan's face fell; his expression grew dark.

"You're right," he said. "That was stupid. *I'm* stupid."

Taylor opened his mouth to reply, but Jon was already disappearing into the tiny bathroom, muttering to himself. Glanced over at his book, Taylor decided against it, and started pacing the room himself. He'd crossed a line. He knew it.

Jonathan was the optimist of the two of them, but these past six months had frayed them both to the breaking point. The truth of their isolation was immense and crushing. There was really no telling what would happen next if Jon didn't come out in a minute or so.

Needing something to focus on, Taylor stepped outside and looked at the street. Zombies were congregating around the front of the building again. One of the first things he and Jon had done was to fortify the entrances with a gauntlet of sharp metal poles. It kept the dead from their doors, but the mindless horde kept shoving forward, impaling themselves on the spikes. Right now, the barrier was clotted with twitching, groaning forms. Later, they could amuse themselves by dropping Molotov cocktails on the horde; it was better than TV used to be.

Jonathan didn't look at Taylor as he came out onto the balcony. In his right hand was their revolver, with its last two bullets. Without reloads for it, those last two shells had taken on grave significance. One for each of them. At the end.

"What are you doing?" Taylor's voice was strident and laced with panic.

"Why are we bothering, Tay?" asked Jon. "Really? What possible outcome is there?

Taylor wanted to rush his friend, try to rip the gun out of his hands, but every single muscle seemed paralyzed. "We've got to go on," he whispered. "We've got to."

"Why?" repeated Jon. He faced Taylor and socked the barrel of the gun into the soft flesh beneath his chin. "Don't worry," said Jonathan, "I won't be back to eat you."

"Don't," said Taylor. He fought to keep from screaming, lest his friend pull the trigger out of reflex.

"I need you," he continued, "I'm not ready to give up. If you do this, though, you might as well shoot me first, because I can't go on without you."

Jonathan gave him a mirthless smile, "I thought I annoyed the piss out of you?"

"You do," blurted Taylor, "But that's what keeps me going." He looked out into the night. The stars were bright, unclouded by streetlights that were long dead.

"If it weren't for our fights, Jon, I'd have jumped over this railing a month ago. You're... everything to me."

Some of the old light flickered in Jonathan's eyes. "Everything?" he asked.

Taylor flushed. Time seemed to stop, and the air grew thick and still between them. Finally, Taylor nodded.

"Everything."

Jonathan lowered the gun, paused, then drew Taylor close and hugged him tight. Things had changed between them now, forever.

They stood embracing for almost a minute. Loving each other. At last, Jonathan pulled back, and whispered in Taylor's ear, "But where's all the skeletons?"

Taylor smiled and punched Jon lightly on the shoulder, wiping away tears. "You dick."

"You love it," Jon replied.

"I guess I do," laughed Taylor. "Want to bomb some zombies?"

"*Cool.*"

THE DOLL MAKER AND THE RAT

Gavin looked up as his doctor entered. He gave a small, dismissive chuckle and went back to looking out the window.

"Back again, huh, doc?"

When there was no reply, he added, "Think this time'll cure me? Get me outta here?"

The doctor inclined his head, seeming pensive, and then said, "You seem to be in a good mood today. That's positive."

Gavin squinted against the sunlight flooding in from the window. He studied the doctor carefully. In turn, the doctor remained silent, waiting for his reply.

Finally, Gavin burst out laughing.

"You're not a real doctor, are you?"

The doctor nodded, then cleared his throat. "We felt," he said, "that you weren't responding to traditional therapies."

"We?" shouted Gavin, "Who's we? You're a fucking rat."

"My," said the rat, "You *are* clear today." It sat back on its haunches and stroked its whiskers.

"It seems a shame to squander this opportunity," continued the rat/doctor. "I'd still like to talk. If you're willing, that is."

Gavin rocked back, resting his head on the wall, and letting the sun from the single window fall on his face. He didn't look at the doctor, but said, "Whatever you want, doc."

"Fine," said the doctor. "How about some word association?"

"You know *all* the games, don't you?" replied Gavin. He sighed and nodded. "Fine. Whatever you'd like."

"Excellent," chirped the rat, "Just say whatever comes into your mind first."

They began:

Hot.
Cold.

Tall.
Short.

Fat.
Disgusting.

Man.
Woman.

Woman.
Girl.

Girl.
Doll.

Doll.
Kill.

Doll.
Evil.

Doll.
Fff... ffu...

Gavin was starting to breathe hard. The world was starting to swim again. He wanted one of his special dollies, the ones without eyes. They couldn't look at him. He'd hold it so tight, and stroke its hair, and everything would be good again.

"That was very good," said the doctor, wiping a sweat from his fur, "Take a rest."

Gavin did.

"Now," continued the doctor, "What do you think it is about dolls that unsettles you so?"

"Their eyes," replied Gavin, almost instantaneously, "Those cold blue eyes that won't stop looking at me."

"I see," said the doctor, twitching his tail back and forth. "And what colour were your mother's eyes, Gavin?"

Gavin didn't reply. Instead, he picked at the scraps on his tin plate. There was a bread crust with a scrap of cheese slice stuck to it. When he'd arrived here, he'd been angry. Defiant, he'd thrown the food back at them, smearing it on the wall day after day. Tiring of that, he'd begun fouling the food, leaving it steaming and stinking by the door. After that, they strapped him down and fed him nutrients through a tube, and he had begun eating again. Eating was never part of the problem; it was their *rules* he hated.

"Would you please answer me, Gavin?" said the doctor, his tone surprisingly forceful for a rat. "What colour were your mother's eyes?"

Gavin knew the answer would just cause trouble, but what could he do? They would just keep asking until he told—merciless bastards. This rodent was no different. He was just another part of their "Wellness" machine.

"Blue," he mumbled.

"I see," said the doctor, scratching his nose, "We're making some real progress here today, Gavin. I'm very proud of you."

"Sure," said Gavin, "Great." He ran his finger around the edge of the tin plate, gathering up potato chip crumbs. Closing his eyes, he sucked the salt off of his fingers.

"Tell me about the buttons, Gavin," said the doctor.

"What?" said Gavin, disturbed from his enjoyment. He'd thought they would continue talking about the Bitch.

The very thought of mother trapped him momentarily in a memory of "discipline time." He'd spilled mother's cup all over the living room floor. In her cold and professional manner, mother had asked him to please meet her in the guest bedroom. It always happened in the guestroom, that sterile, not-for-you torture chamber, where mother's doll collection resided. Row upon row of baby-doll eyes watched while Mother took up her short green-handled whip and peeled flesh from his pubescent back. His screams falling upon dozens of sets of uncaring china ears, and one set that was simply inhuman.

Gavin stood up and looked out the window. At least the view here was all right. Warm yellow sunshine painted the expansive lawn a violent, vibrant green. The sight cheered him, and brought him back to now, where the "doctor" was growing inpatient.

"It seems we lost you for a minute there," said the doctor. While Gavin had been lost in thought, the rat had climbed the vinyl padding and now sat perched on the windowsill. Seeing the rat mere inches from his face made him retreat a few steps.

Unfazed, the rat continued, "What were you thinking about just now, Gavin? Was it your mother?"

"Yeah," admitted Gavin, turning away.

"Would you like to talk about it?"

"No."

"All right then. Let's continue talking about the buttons."

"The doctor last week knew all this stuff." said Gavin, hating the sulky tone he heard in his own voice.

"Enlighten me as well then," said the doctor, with a tone of unyielding, condescending patience. He repeated the next slowly, and each word was a spike between Gavin's eyes, "Tell. Me. About. The. Buttons."

It was enough. Enough questions, enough tests. Gavin lunged at the doctor. He let loose a feral shriek, preparing to bite the doctor in two if he could manage it.

The doctor squealed, and jumped off the windowsill, then darted to the door.

Gavin's momentum carried him face first into the wall. Padded or not... it hurt. He cried out in pain and sat down hard.

Cowering now, the doctor stared at Gavin with his queer black eyes, and squeaked, "That was unnecessary."

Rubbing his throbbing and bleeding nose, Gavin said, "You were bullying me. I hate bullies."

His voice still high and panicked, the doctor tried to regain composure, saying, "You might have simply told me that."

Shaking his head, both in negation, and to clear the cobwebs, Gavin said, "That was more fun," and managed a smile.

Walking cautiously along the wall—and out of reach— the doctor tried again, "What do you suggest we do instead, Gavin?" It inched a little closer, "Sooner or later, you're going to have to think about what you did."

Images spun in Gavin's mind: matted hair, wet, choked screams, and his blade pushing past resisting skin and flicking out that which offended him. His fingers remembered the hard press of the needle as he sewed big button eyes on to his dollies. His dollies were for touching. His dollies were the perfect playmates, after their nasty blue eyes were gone. They were quiet, pliable, and lovely. He made sure to hug them all goodnight before he left them propped up against the pillows. Now, though, there were no more dollies. There was only this cell, this window, and a rat.

"I don't know, Doc. Maybe I should just off myself?"

The Doctor nodded, "Now *that* is an interesting suggestion."

Gavin gave a snort of involuntary laughter. "That's not very doctor-like of you, is it? Aren't you supposed to be trying to save me?"

The Doctor made a small clicking, chewing sound in his throat, then cleared it with a tiny but perfectly human "ahem". Coming to the middle of the floor, it looked up and said, "I'm saying, Gavin, that if you refuse to discuss your crimes, you aren't going to get any better and you'll stay here until you die."

Gavin didn't answer. He couldn't. Bizarre as this whole thing was, the rodent was right.

"And if that's the case," continued Dr. Rat, "Today is as good a day to die as ten years from now, isn't it?"

Scratching his right bicep, where the whitecoats always jabbed their damned "calm-down" needles, Gavin considered, then said, "So, what, you've got a better idea?"

There was a long silence. Gavin considered.

"Just go with it," suggested the rat, "It can only help."

Laughing, Gavin said to himself, "It'll help. Maybe. Except now, I'm talking to rats."

"What are you going to do?" said the rat with a shrug, "We've all got problems. I'm bipolar."

"Really?" asked Gavin, "How's that?"

"Awful," said the rat, walking over to the remains of Gavin's lunch.

"Are you going to eat that?"

DEVIL'S NIGHT

The glass door swung open, and Jason jumped down the three steps, prize under his arm. He flipped the six-pack of toilet paper up in the air with his right hand. It turned end over end and Jason made a showy, dipping catch with his left hand. Derek was unimpressed.

"Why'd you get the expensive brand?" he asked. "We're not wiping our asses with it."

"What the hell does the brand matter?" replied Jason, holding the package out in front of him. "I didn't even look at the different kinds."

"Dude, the brand *doesn't* matter," Derek added. "We only had ten bucks, and you just spent six of it so the trees can, what, feel the soft little kittens between their branches?"

"Oh," replied Jason. "Shit."

"I guess we can forget about the spray paint." He didn't like cutting Jason down, but this wasn't the first time the big goof had spoiled their plans by doing something stupid.

Jason stood in front of the convenience store steps, the bag with the toilet paper drooping from one finger at his side. "Sorry, man."

Derek looked at him for a second longer. He shook his head, letting it go. Jason looked pathetic. And besides, it would take a lot to get him down tonight. He lit another smoke on the cherry of his own, and gave it to Jason, saying, "Forget it, dude. Let's get going—it's already eleven-thirty."

Over the next forty-five minutes, Jason redeemed himself, hitting on the perfect technique to get the TP super high up in the trees without breaking. The trick, he demonstrated, was to double up the first two feet or so, before lobbing the rest of the roll high into the air.

"It doesn't hurt," said Jason, watching a long trail of paper flutter from a nearly naked oak branch, "that we're using the good stuff. Three quilted plies, man. That's good paper." Derek had to laugh.

Later, when the last roll was spent, pumpkin after pumpkin soared high over the street to explode with a giggle-inducing hollow crunch. Some of the gourds met their end beneath the soles of Derek's steel-toed work boots, his *stompers*. Their funny faces bulged in dismay as he brought his feet down on their hollow heads.

Derek stopped in the middle of the street and rested his hands on his knees. He was starting to feel that, just maybe, the smokes were not the best idea he'd ever had.

"You crappin' out already?" Jason laughed. He changed his grip on the pumpkin he was holding.

It had come from Mr. Ellison's porch. The old man was forever yelling at all the kids to get away from his yard, yet, on Halloween, he always decorated his house. The large front porch pumpkin, however, had not been carved.

"Watch this one," said Jason, heaving the head-sized gourd overhand. It struck the sharp edge of the concrete porch steps, releasing a shower of orange pulp that spattered like rain on Ellison's puke green door. A light came on inside the house.

Jason and Derek ran behind the bushes across the street. Derek pulled a single bough aside and took a look. Jason, meanwhile, was fumbling with something in his pockets.

"What are you *doing*?" asked Derek.

In reply, Jason produced his cell phone and aimed it through the opening in the bush. "TikTok," he whispered. "I should've thought of this earlier."

Ellison's door opened. A moment later, the man himself was on the porch, honking and sputtering about "frigging kids." Jason had a hand cupped over his mouth. His shoulders hitched up and down and his face was turning red. Ellison came running into the middle of the street, threadbare slippers slapping against the pavement, bellowing about calling the police. Jason was so intent on the filtered image in his phone that he didn't notice Ellison turning toward them. Derek snatched the phone out of his hands, and the bush closed soundlessly. From the house next door came a shout to "shut the hell up, Ellison."

Several minutes passed and, finally, Ellison gave up and went back inside. The moment the puke-green door slammed shut, Derek and Jason crept slowly between the houses behind them, and on to the next street over. They paused, looked at each other, and burst out laughing.

"*You damned kids...*" Jason croaked in an eerie imitation of the old man. That got them going again. Derek had to rub his pumpkin-sludge covered hands off on his jeans just so he could wipe the tears from his eyes.

***

It was two o'clock when, covered with tiny pumpkin chunks and bits of toilet paper, they arrived at the end of Laurelin Drive and stood staring up a sloped lawn to the old Johnson place. It was actually the new Reynolds' place, but their suburb was small and old enough that everyone still thought of it as the Johnson place.

Derek thumped Jay on the back. "Come on, one more house. One more. We'll call it a night after that."

"Look at that pumpkin," said Jason, pointing. The jack-o'-lantern wasn't the biggest they'd seen that night, but it sat on an elaborate stand of purple tentacles. The porch itself was covered in fake cobwebs, hanging rubber spiders, and various other decorations. Even the idiotic little gnomes in the garden were dressed in costumes. Whoever this Reynolds guy was, he was a total nut for Halloween—and had way too much time on his hands.

"Let's get it," said Derek, flushed as much with excitement as with their exertions.

"Nah," said Jason, his smile faltering, "I don't think that's a good idea. I heard the guy's an alien."

"What?" Derek stopped as if Jason had slapped him. This was the dumbest thing he'd ever heard. From Jason, that was saying something. "Are you an idiot? The guy's name is Reynolds, not *Lopez*."

"That's not cool dude," said Jason. His expression was almost comic in its reproach. "Don't be racist."

"Well, don't be an ass. What are you talking about?"

Jason frowned and looked at the house again. Scratching his dirty brown hair, he said, "He's not *that* kind of alien. He's a *real* alien."

Derek didn't know what to say. He looked into Jason's eyes and saw he was serious. When he found his voice, he said, "You're not normal, Jason. You can't even make up a good ghost story." He shook his head. "What do space aliens have to do with Halloween?"

Even under the yellow streetlight, it was easy to see Jason was turning a deep shade of red.

"Look," he sputtered, "I *know* what Cathy Masovi told me." He gestured to a bungalow two houses to the right, "She lives right there, and she told me that house was empty for, like, three years. Then, back in spring, after that weird lightning storm—you know, the one that lasted for, like, two days?" Derek nodded. Jason continued. "Mr. Reynolds was just *there*. No one saw moving trucks or *nothing*."

Derek zeroed in on the most important piece of news. "When were you talking to Cathy Masovi?"

Jason looked back at the porch, at that weird, flickering jack-o'-lantern. "It was George Naylor's party last week," said Jason. "You were there."

"Yeah," said Derek, "But I don't remember seeing Cathy there."

Jason laughed. "You were so juiced, you weren't seeing much."

"Shut up," replied Derek, "I'd have noticed if Cathy Masovi was there." Derek suddenly felt tired—tired of having to explain everything twice, tired of overlooking the bigger boy's constant dumb mistakes. All the same, he was curious about anything that had to do with Cathy Masovi. He only shared Phys. Ed with the popular brunette, but that was enough. The thought of her in gym shorts was enough to make him start breathing heavily.

"What else did you talk about?" Derek had been trying to get with Cathy for the whole year, and in one night, Jason had said more to her than Derek could manage in an entire semester of Calculus. Before Jason answered, Derek added, "Did she say anything about me?"

"Nah, man, we talked about Halloween and shit. She said her little sister was doing a lame haunted house thing for her friends, and Cathy was getting all these ideas off the internet. I said I wished there was a *real* haunted house, and she…"

Derek cut him off. "Did you get with her?" The entire night was on the verge of being ruined. If his friend had moved on the girl that he wanted for himself… he didn't know what he'd do. Fight? He couldn't take Jason in a fight. Then, on the heels of that thought, he felt a little sick, and that feeling of being tired came back stronger. This was *Jason*. There should never be a reason to fight his best friend. But—if Jason had made out with Cathy…

A low whooping noise from down the street split the stillness of the night, and they both jumped. Strobing blue and red light flashed across their faces and the front of the Reynolds house. Before they could run for it, the police cruiser had pulled up in front of them.

"That conversation isn't over," said Derek under his breath, then shut up as a thoroughly unimpressed police officer got out of the car and walked toward them, shining a flashlight right in their faces.

"What are you boys doing out so late?" Her tone demanded the absolute truth.

The truth, however, was not what was going to get them out of this, at least not the *whole* truth. Derek cut a quick look at Jason, who returned the look with a quick, almost non-existent nod. He'd keep his mouth shut, and Derek would talk them out of trouble—just like always.

"We heard someone out here," said Derek. He gave her his best *good student* smile. "My friend had his bike stolen last month. We thought maybe the guys had come back for his new one. It sounded like they ran this way."

"It's three in the morning," said the cop. "It's a school night, and you're together. You'll have to do better than that."

"We were watching movies," blurted Jason. Derek stared at him. *What the fuck was he doing?* He was going to screw them both trying to "help", but Derek couldn't say anything now. He'd have to go with Jay's story, or they'd be done.

"Movies?" repeated the officer.

"Yeah," said Jason, warming up, "We've been at it all week. Every year, me and Derek watch all the Friday the 13th movies in a row. We do it every year." He gulped a little at the end, realizing he was babbling, perhaps. The cop didn't notice, though.

"And that took you until three in the morning?" She smelled something funny about their story, Derek knew it. But she didn't have anything to base it on yet. Derek became very aware of the pumpkin pulp that was covering the bottom of his boots. He was glad that he was standing on the grass. The cop was still looking at him with the same expression of annoyed expectation.

Derek gambled, "We, um… were downloading the new one from the internet. We finished number twelve and got carried away, I guess. Anyway, while we were waiting for it to come, I heard some guys out here, and when we looked out my window…"

"We saw three kids out smashing people's pumpkins and shit," Jason finished.

"Don't say shit in front of a policeman, asshole," snapped Derek, slugging Jason in the arm.

"Sorry, D."

"Hold on." The cop had put her flashlight away. "Knock it off." Her tone was shifting from suspicion to exasperation. She looked over at Jason. "Did you see the kids who were breaking pumpkins?"

"Not really. Sorry," said Jason. "It sounded like there were what, three of them? Derek?"

Derek nodded.

"Yeah, three," Jason went on, "One of 'em is a girl."

"I'm still not sure that it wasn't you two," the cop said, looking hard at Derek now. Her eyes narrowed, and to his amazement, she smiled. It was a cold, cynical smile. "What number is the Friday the 13th movie where they're on a boat?"

"Number eight," said Derek. Jason's choice of movie to lie about, at least, was bang on. Jason was a freak for the horror movies featuring his namesake, and Derek had, indeed, sat through most of them several times as well. "Jason takes Manhattan."

"It's the least bloody of the bunch though," Jason chimed in. "We skip to the good parts in that one—there's only about twenty minutes of good stuff—like the part where this guy gets his head punched off and it *totally* looks like a Styrofoam dummy head and…."

"All right. Shut up." The cop sighed. "Look. I'm not seeing anything right now that shows you've been disturbing the neighbourhood." They started to relax, and she stopped them with a look. "I'm not saying you *didn't*. You probably *did*. But it's not worth me trying to prove it."

She lowered her flashlight. "So," she continued, "This is your one get-out-of-trouble-free card. But you're going to do two things."

Looking at Jason, the cop said, "You're going to go straight home. Without stopping. And I'm not going to see either of you on these streets after midnight again."

Moving her gaze to Derek, she added, "And if you're telling the truth about downloading movies, I'd suggest you erase them all." She paused, perhaps taking the time of day into consideration, and finished, "Tomorrow."

"Okay. Yeah." Derek said. "I will as soon as I get home, okay?"

"Fine," said the cop. "And that's right now, correct?"

They nodded.

The officer got back in her cruiser. She sat, watching them, until they started moving. Derek started up Reynolds' driveway. Feeling the cop still looking at them, he popped Jason on the arm again. This time, Jason pushed him back. He was playing along, though, and didn't push hard.

The cop didn't bother with the siren. Instead, she gave a single blast on the horn. When they looked back, they saw her behind the wheel, shaking a finger at them. They nodded in tandem, as if finishing a performance. The act, however, was a success, and the cruiser backed away and rolled up the street.

Derek pulled out the smokes. His hand was trembling a bit. That had been too close. He offered Jason a cigarette. Jason took it, and they lit up.

Jason stopped where he was on the driveway. He was looking at the decorations again. "Man," he said, "This stuff is *crazy*."

"Yeah," Derek said. "Weird." He wasn't done talking about Cathy Masovi yet. He tapped Jason on the shoulder. When Jason turned, Derek continued, "Look, did you kiss her? Or what? Something?"

No reply. The moment dragged out long enough for Derek's suspicions to take hold. Jason's lip curled up into a sneer. "Get over it, man. We just *talked*."

"You fucking liar," said Derek. He kept his voice low, but only because he was trying very hard not to yell. The anger had welled up from nowhere. But here it was, and he wanted *answers*.

"Why'd you hesitate? You were *with* her. Admit it."

"Fine," said Jason. His tone was cold. "I kissed her. Happy? She kissed me back too."

"How could you do that to me?" Derek's voice was rising, on the verge of becoming a whine. He was afraid he'd start shouting in a minute, which would land them right back in trouble. For the moment, he didn't care. He took a step forward. Jason didn't move.

"Look, don't you put any of this on me, D," said Jason. "If you're so into her, try *talking* to her tomorrow, or maybe, I don't know, ask her out?" His own voice was rising, and Derek looked up at the still –dark upper windows of Reynolds' house. They'd been in front of this guy's house way too long. If the guy came out, the cop would be the least of their worries. Picking a fight with Jason right now was idiotic.

"All right, " he said. "I'm sorry, man." He held out a hand to stop Jay from replying. "You're right. I should've manned up by now. Let's forget it, okay?" Jason brightened a bit, and Derek added, "And we *both* have to keep quiet—we're going to bring this guy running outside any minute."

Jason started, as if he'd temporarily forgotten that they were in someone else's yard.

Looking over his shoulder at the front door, Jason said, "Yeah. Let's go." He started walking toward the little gate.

Now that their second crisis was passing behind them, Derek started to think back on the night's activities and had an idea. What they needed to do was end the night on a high. Something to erase the last twenty minutes.

"Let's still do this house, though. Okay?" he asked. "One more for the road. Huh?"

Jason stopped. "I dunno, man." He looked at the jack-o'-lantern again. "I don't like the look of this stuff."

Standing and smoking, Derek had a wicked thought, that making Jason wreck that freaky pumpkin would kind of make up for him being an ass with the cop, and maybe a bit of the Cathy Masovi thing, too.

"Come on," he said, "Don't puss out now. We did a dozen pumpkins, and we're going to leave the dumbest looking one on the block alone?"

"Last house," said Jason. It wasn't a question. Derek nodded.

"Go get that pumpkin. I'm going to go trash those gnomes."

"The cop?" asked Jason, cocking an eyebrow.

"It'll take us two seconds. Less if you start now. *Go!*" Jason went. Derek took a deep breath. It felt, for the moment, as if the natural order of things had returned to normal.

Taking two quick steps, Jason mounted the steps. He paused, looking at the bannister.

"These lights are *weird, man*," he said. "They look like plants, with leaves and stuff."

Derek didn't answer. He turned and started walking toward the gnomes. Probably he'd only kick them over and throw their stupid little hats into the bushes or something. He was starting to drag—three a.m. was around the corner and, weekend or not, it had been a very long evening.

Bending down, he picked up one of the ceramic statues that had been draped with a tiny sheet. With the pointy hat underneath, the effect was of the world's tiniest Klansman. *This'll serve the Reynolds guy right*, thought Derek. The statue was heavier than it seemed. He started to swing it back, meaning to toss it hard over the low hedge into the road, when Jason made a funny sound behind him, and he turned.

"This thing feels *weird*, man," came Jason's voice. Derek wanted to yell at him to shut up, but that would've defeated the purpose. A moment later, he started to laugh. Jason was dancing around on the porch with the odd jack-o'-lantern. The weird purple stand seemed to be attached to it. Jason twirled his partner around twice, ripping down some of the thick clots of cobweb material in the process.

"Here we go Derek!" Jason called, the pumpkin held high over his head. "Watch this one!"

In the next instant, everything changed.

Derek thought for a moment that there was some weird light effect that they'd missed so far. It looked as if the purple pumpkin stand had come *alive* somehow. Jason's scream came floating across the yard, and Derek bolted toward the porch. The tentacles convulsed and pulled the pumpkin down on top of Jason's head. The result was almost comical in spite of his horrified shrieks.

A light went on inside the house, and Derek skidded to a stop. For a brief moment, Derek's sense of self–preservation warred with his instinct to help his friend. He turned toward the sidewalk. To his alarm, the low picket fence seemed to have grown by at least two feet, and the shrubs that separated Reynolds' lawn from the other two houses seemed to have gotten larger as well. The gate was now a brief glimpse of rusted iron through a deep cleft in the hedge. Derek couldn't remember having seen thorns—at least not ones that large—on the bushes when they passed through, either.

Jason flailed, turning to face Derek. He could see no sign at all of the boy's head through the cut –outs in the pumpkin. Even so, the air was still thick with muffled cries of distress. Derek charged across the lawn and up the steps. He seized hold of the jack-o'-lantern. It was repulsive to the touch, smooth and loose like the skin of a diseased frog. The thick, pulpy mouth began working up and down, catching his index finger between its strange orange lips, and Derek felt something like teeth poke into his skin. With an enormous lurch, he pulled his hand free and staggered back.

That was the moment the rest of the decorations came to life. A full-sized skeleton that hung from the door began to dance. It clicked and clacked as its bony limbs clattered against the door, pushing itself free of the brass hook that had held it in place. Tumbling to the ground with a sound like dice in a cup, the skeleton began to clamber to its feet. Derek backed away and felt resistance.

Long gossamer strands of cobweb detached from the eaves and began to brush against Derek's back, sides, and head. Where they touched, they stuck and became stiff. Before he knew what was happening, he was held in place, and the skeleton was almost upright now. He clawed at the strands, but they had become as unyielding as steel cable. All was silent. Jason had stopped struggling. Derek looked over and saw that his friend was standing bolt upright. The pumpkin-head tipped forward and began to suction-walk its way down Jason's body. The boy's head was gone. There was no blood. The lights from the living room window illuminated a shiny pink-white sheet of skin that ran from shoulder to shoulder. A moment later, the body sank to its knees and slammed forward onto the floor. Derek screamed. More strands floated down to silence him, and Derek clapped his hands over his mouth, denying them entry. The slender cords attached to the backs of his hands, stinging with miserable fire. The skeleton had gained its legs, and now took a step toward him, arms outstretched.

From the deck behind him, Derek heard a new noise. It sounded like rocks scraping on wood. Derek twisted around in time to see tiny hands reaching up over the bannister. A miniature pointed witch's hat preceded a maniacal chiselled stone face over the handrail. The garden gnomes, all three of them, were coming to join the party. Derek didn't want to know what they were going to do.

In the next moment, the front porch was flooded with light, as "Mr. Reynolds" walked out, taking little shuffling, hopping steps. He was a short, hunched old man, wearing what looked like a bad Ronald Reagan mask. There was something funny about the mask, though. It didn't seem to end at his neckline. The hunched little man tottered closer, studying Derek. Mr. Reynolds smiled, or rather, the rubber mask formed a grotesque approximation of a smile. Derek whimpered, trying to blink away the salty tears streaming from his eyes. With a slow grinding sound that made his skin itch, the garden gnomes swivelled their stone heads to look at their master. Reynolds' eyes flashed with sick purple light, and the gnomes dropped back down over the railing. There were three muffled thuds as they hit the ground. The skeleton's slow, deliberate journey had come to an end at last, and Derek thought he could feel a wave of malevolent joy as its bony fingers settled on his shoulders.

Reynolds hop-walked forward and grasped the skeleton by the back of the neck. With an effortless movement of his arm, he back-handed the pile of bones through the open door behind it. Reynolds made a noise like cicadas screaming.

Derek struggled, still trying to free himself from the web.

"Oh. Dear me," said Mr. Reynolds. His tone was a clicking mechanical singsong.

"Is it Halloween already? I thought it was tomorrow for some reason." Patting at the rubber mask, he said, "My disguise is not even ready yet."

Reynolds's gaze fell on the headless corpse that had recently been Jason. "My goodness, fellows, it seems that my festive spirit has been a trifle… aggressive." Turning back to Derek, he continued, "Nonetheless, I do wish I'd had one more night to prepare." He reached down and stroked the pumpkin. The thing's eyes flashed the same sick purple as the man's own had behind the mask. The odd little gourd started purring. Derek wanted to throw up.

With another grotesque rubber grin, Reynolds continued, "There's no accounting, I suppose, for the impetuousness of youth." Derek listened to the thing's stilted language and cursed himself that he'd ever doubted Jason. The man blinked behind his mask and Derek saw a scaly blue eyelid with a thin, opaque membrane that jittered across the surface.

"Still," continued Reynolds, "You boys will want your tricks and treats, I suppose. Don't go anywhere." He went back into the house with his weird shuffling, bobbing gait. Derek thrashed with renewed fervour against the petrified gossamer that held him and managed to get his left hand free. As the strands popped off his flesh, they ripped chunks out of his clothing and scored his skin. The pain from a dozen tiny wounds was excruciating, but he bit his lip against his cries, and willed Reynolds to take more time. With a final wrenching twist, Derek fell flat to the floor of the porch, coming face to stump with the headless bulk of his friend.

Light washed across his face as the door opened again. "Dear me," the thing said in its inhuman voice, "you are more precocious than I thought." Reynolds stood silhouetted against the brightness from within. "You have *certainly* earned your tricks and treats." He was holding a tray in his hands.

He shuffle-hopped closer and crouched by Derek. "The young ones where I come from love these." He placed the tray on the ground. Derek looked at the platter and made a low grunt of disgust. The things looked like dark green caterpillars with broad stripes of violent pink, and with a single large eye on a stalk that grew straight up from one end. Derek shoved himself to his knees, and from there, tried to get to his feet. Reynolds's hand darted forward and caught him.

"Stay. I insist. It is only polite."

"What *are* they?" Derek asked, trying to pull away, but the hand was even stronger than the threads had been, and he was forced into a sitting position. The hairs on his neck stood up with horror as he realized that when he'd spoken, all the tiny creatures' eyes had swayed on their stalks in his direction. They were *listening* to him.

Reynolds said, "These are excellent tricks and treats. The *trick* is to eat them…" He stroked the back of one of the caterpillars. It reared up off the tray at his touch, and Derek saw that its entire underside was composed of tiny, sharp teeth. He popped the one he'd been petting into his mouth. "… Before they eat you."

The sound of the man-thing chewing behind his mask was too much for Derek. He grabbed at the hand that was holding him and dug in with his fingernails. The middle two fingers came away in his hand, ripped away like tissue paper. Where they'd been, a ragged hole in the man's rubbery flesh revealed more lumpy blue scales and the start of a horny purple talon.

Derek drew both legs up to his chest and rocked back. Something hard in his back pocket pressed into him. He kicked out hard with both feet and hit Reynolds square in the chest. Surprise was on his side, and he was free. Derek jumped to his feet and found that the cobweb tendrils were in motion again, blocking the stairs to the lawn. The jack-o'-lantern prevented him from going over the edge of the railing, and Reynolds was already recovering from the blow. His butt twitched where he'd sat down funny. It was the lighter. Shoving his hand into his pocket, Derek came up with the purple Bic and flicked the wheel. It flicked sparks once, twice, and then it was lit. There wasn't any reason to believe that the alien material would be flammable, but it was all Derek had. He touched the tiny flame to the nearest cobweb he could reach. The reaction was immediate. The entire mass went up in seconds, creating a flash of light and flame that was painful to look at. From behind him came an ear-splitting shriek of pain. Mr. Reynolds, it seemed, didn't like fire either. Derek turned and saw the man–thing stagger back into the house, an arm thrown across its eyes. Luck paid Derek one final favour, and the thickest ends of the cobwebs, where they were attached to the house, took longer to burn, and the flame spread out, lapping at the old wood of the porch. Derek's right foot flared with pain. He looked down and saw one of the carnivorous candy-worms attached to his boot. It had worked its way through the leather instep in seconds, and he could feel its myriad teeth against his skin. Not stopping to think, he slammed the thing against the side of the newel post, and the worm burst. Its tiny eye popped free and landed among the rest of the "treats", which made quick work of it.

Reynolds was screaming what could only be obscenities in its guttural, awful language. The entire porch was in flames, and Derek was standing in shock on the lawn. The shape of the man thing moved back into the house. With a huge rending crack, the front beam of the porch fell down, burning embers spewing everywhere as it hit the ground. He dashed toward the gate. To his horror, one of the psychotic little gnomes was crawling toward him on its cement belly. Derek screamed and kicked the freakish thing with all his strength. Its head exploded on contact with the steel-toed boot, sending a small shower of plaster and paint flying across the lawn. The gnome's torso collapsed to the ground, and thick, red liquid began to pour from its ragged neck.

Without looking back, Derek ran down the small path, and forced his way through the overgrown hedge. Thorns caught and tore his shirt. He ignored the deep scratches and kept going. He leapt over the small garden gate, but his foot caught the top edge as he sailed over, and he fell down hard on the sidewalk. The world swam out of focus. Behind him, on the lawn, Derek could hear movement. Through the haze of his fading consciousness, he remembered that there had been several other gnomes, and that he couldn't assume any of them had been caught up in the blaze on the porch. As if to confirm his fears, he heard a tiny *plink* as concrete feet reached the pathway. He ran. Pain throbbed in a dozen places on his body: his shoulders still burned from the touch of the cobweb, his calf hurt where that weird caterpillar–thing had bitten him and his skin felt hot and tight all over from being so near the fire. Now his knees and forehead were an agony of scraped and oozing flesh.

As he reached the end of the street, his clomping boots weighing three pounds each at least, Derek started to slow up. His mind was already beginning to replay the horrors he'd witnessed, and he shook his head as if the thoughts were a physical thing, clinging to his scalp, that he could hope to fling off. The movement made his growing headache worse. He didn't care. If he thought too long about what had happened, he felt he might stop where he was and start screaming at the sky. So, he moved, and tried to think of nothing.

Fifteen minutes later, Derek found himself standing at the door in back of his house, the one that led downstairs to the basement, and his bedroom. He was startled. The walk home was a blank, he couldn't recall making any turns or even looking at any street names. His feet had brought him to the right place, regardless. Derek fumbled his shaking hands into his pockets, meaning to get his keys, open this door, go downstairs, and fall asleep. Sleep was what he wanted most of all. He must be in shock. How could he not be? If he could sleep, though, he might stand at least a small chance of making sense of everything in the morning. His hands came up empty, no keys.

This final, small problem was one thing too many. Derek turned around, slid down the door and sat hugging his knees. He began to cry. His shoulders shook with huge, gasping sobs, as he wept for Jason, for himself, for having endured something that should not even exist. An unknowable time later, his head came to rest on his knees, and he fell asleep.

***

"Derek! What the hell are you doing out here?"

Coming roughly awake, Derek rubbed his swollen eyes. His father was shaking him by the arm. The raw patches on his skin where Reynolds' awful web had stuck to him screamed at the touch, and he jerked back. He looked up into his father's face. Martin Collins' expression was a mixture of anger and concern. For a moment, Derek couldn't remember anything.

"What? How did I… where…"

"That's what I want to know," said his dad. "Why the hell are you out here?"

The night started flooding back, and Derek felt his guts turn hollow again. What could he possibly say? From the look on his face, Martin's patience, thin to begin with, was nearing its end.

"I lost my keys," said Derek, starting with the obvious.

"All right," his father replied. His tone was calm. Too calm. "Why didn't you knock?"

Derek opened his mouth to speak, but his dad kept going, "Jesus, Derek, we thought you were in bed. The next thing we know, it's six a.m. and you're not home. We were worried sick."

"I… I mean we…" Derek stammered. Where could he possibly begin?

Martin's lips drew down at the corners.

"We?" he repeated. "You mean Jason, right?"

"Yeah," said Derek.

"Get in the house," his father said. His tone had gone dry, and authoritative. "Whenever you and that idiot get together, it's trouble. I'm *sick* of it."

"Dad," Derek began.

"Save it," snapped Martin. "Go to your room. Get some sleep. You're grounded."

"Grounded?" asked Derek, "Dad, you don't understand…"

"I understand you're about eight hours past your curfew." He started walking into the house. The conversation was over. Derek watched him walk into the house, wanting to scream the words that were pounding in time with his pulse. *Jason's dead, Jason's dead, Jason's DEAD.* Who could he call for help? How could he *begin* to explain?

"In the house," called Martin. *"Now."*

***

Derek didn't sleep.

***

If his father had wanted to torture him, Derek thought, this was the way to do it. He was ready to beat his head against the wall to stop the thoughts of the night before from coming back. "Grounded" meant no TV, no phone calls, and no internet, but Derek had booted up his laptop, and gone to the local news site, keeping the volume muted. He needed to see if there would be anything about the fire. More than that, he wanted to see if there would be anything about Jason. He'd resigned himself that if he saw the slightest word about the incident, then he would call the police himself. The problem was—what if nothing *had* happened? But then, *where was Jason?* After ninety minutes, the headlines of the day had been updated four times, and still there was nothing about the destruction of a suburban house the night before.

If there was no fire, where's Jason? Where was I? His pulse was throbbing in his temples. At noon, when his mother knocked on the door to bring in a sandwich, Derek had screamed. *Screamed.* He wondered again if this was what insanity felt like. His mind began to fill the shadow in his room with sick images of the concrete gnomes with their rigid, homicidal grins. He opened the shade all the way and turned on all the lights. He played music, he read books. Nothing worked. He checked the computer again. There was one new email—from *screaminjayjay99@gmail.ca*. Derek clicked on it. His hand was trembling, and he closed the window by mistake. He tried again. The message was brief.

D,

Was that a crazy nite, or what??? Wickid headache today. Why'd you leave so quick? Talk 2 you tonite, k? Got something *awesome* to show you.

J.

The blood drained from his face. Derek thought he was going to pass out. If Jason was alive and emailing—what did that say about the rest of the evening? Had they taken drugs at one point? He didn't remember—but if they were strong enough… He just didn't know. There was no way he could call the police now.

Martin opened the door. Derek jumped. He rolled his seat back against the wall.

"Turn that computer off, you're grounded," said Martin. There was nothing menacing in his tone—it was an automatic response to "the rules" being bent. It was such a *normal*, if unwelcome, thing to say that Derek almost smiled. Instead, he reached over and closed the lid on the laptop.

"Your mother and I are going out tonight," his father continued. "You'll have to give out the candy."

When no answer came, Martin frowned. He stepped into the room and took a long look at Derek.

"Son," said Martin, "I don't know what you were up to last night, but your mother says you seem *different* today, edgy."

"It was… a bad night," Derek said, trying to keep the panic from his voice.

"Are you in trouble?" asked his father, his gaze sharpening. *"Police trouble?"*

"No." Derek said. "We—I mean—it was late, and we saw some stuff that was kind of scary." *Like killer garden gnomes, a killer skeleton and a pumpkin that eats heads. And let's not forget my best friend, who may or may not be dead.*

"Look," said Martin, "I was young once too, and the streets can get a little crazy after midnight. That's one of the reasons you have a curfew." He looked at Derek for a long moment, seeming to weigh his next words carefully. "Look," he said, "give the candy out tonight. We'll talk about being grounded tomorrow, all right? You can tell me your story then, too. Deal?"

Derek's fevered thoughts jumped back to the first thing his father had said, "Wait. You guys are leaving me alone?" Derek was breathing hard, and his forehead was clammy with sweat.

"It's a bunch of *kids* Derek." Martin's moment of sympathy, if that's what it had been, was gone. "Grow up."

***

That night, the rain hadn't let up, but it wasn't storming hard enough to deter the horde of candy–mad children from doing their thing. His parents went out to their party, leaving Derek to answer the constant ringing of the doorbell. He made the trip dozens of times, giving handfuls of junk to each little troll, Transformer, and witch. Hopefully, he'd run out of treats, and he could shut off the lights soon.

There was another knock on the door. Upon answering, Derek was greeted by a three–foot tall grey alien, staring up at him with big black eyes, and saying "Trick–or–treat."

Derek almost fainted. The kid, after waiting about five seconds, reached into the candy bowl and grabbed a handful of Twix bars, before saying "Thank you" and running off into the night. Derek's heart was pounding again.

It was too much. After a moment or two of painful silence, when all he could hear was the throbbing of his pulse in his ears, Derek decided to get a little something to help him calm down. He went into the kitchen and took his dad's bottle of vodka from the freezer. Holding the bottle to his lips, he took a long, cold swig. The liquor burned his throat, and he coughed. He almost dropped the bottle before steadying himself. He re-capped the booze and put it back. When he got back to the living room, Friday the 13th Part Four had come back from commercial. Jason was on the hunt again. Several minutes passed in blissful eighties schlock horror mindlessness. Already he was feeling a bit light-headed.

The doorbell rang.

Derek got up, deciding this time to make some twelve-year-old's night by dumping the entire bowl of fun-sized Mars bars into the kid's pillowcase and be done with it.

He opened the door and was too shocked even to scream. The pumpkin that sat atop Jason's shoulders said, in Jason's voice, "Good evening, Derek."

There was a burst of warmth as hot piss ran down Derek's leg. He opened his mouth, but nothing came out but, "Wh-what?"

"Tonight is Hallow-ween, is it not?" asked Jason. The cadences were Reynolds'.

"You can't be here," Derek managed. "You're…"

"Dead?" asked Jason. "Part of us was destroyed. Yes. That was painful and most… impolite." The pulpy face of the pumpkin broadened into a sagging, rotten smile. "But we are not dead."

Derek's shock faded, and he began to weep. "Why are you doing this to me?"

"It should be obvious," said Jason-not-Jason. "You know our secrets." As he spoke, the flannel shirt that Jason had been wearing last night rippled and bulged in various places. There was no telling what was going on under there.

"Please," said Derek. "Please, let me go. No one will believe me, anyway. Just… *Just go away!*" He was screaming now. The Jason-thing smiled.

"Please? That is not what you must say tonight."

Seizing on that last as a final opportunity to live, Derek cried, "What? What do I need to say? Tell me. I'll say it. I'll do it!"

The pumpkin grin spread wider. Jason began to unbutton his shirt. His bare chest beneath was coated with hundreds of the carnivorous worms. Derek started screaming and didn't stop. Terror had driven all rational thought from his mind. His head was filled with bright white fuzz that seemed to press against his face from the inside. All that he had left in the world was his voice, and his scream. It was so loud, so consistent, that he failed to hear the Jason-thing's final words:

"Trick… or… Treat?"

PICK YOUR OWN PUMPKIN

"Can we get some more light out here?"

Milton tried again to get the attention of the uniform who was sitting in the passenger seat of his car. The man's face was ash pale.

"Officer?"

The man looked up, seeming to finally hear.

"P-Power's out. We radioed for them to bring the big Kliegs and Gennies out, but they're twenty minutes away."

He put his head down, hands gripping the dash. "Jesus, detective. You ever seen…"

"Yeah." Milton nodded, grim. "This one's up there, though." He ran a hand through his hair. "But it's all the same crime. Dead is dead."

The officer didn't answer, so Milton crossed the barnyard to revisit the grotesque wall of jack-o'-lanterns. Window dressing or not, the killer had gone to a lot of trouble. There were three rows of ten pumpkins, stacked one on the other, each carved into a goofy grin, sinister smirk, or—most chilling to Al—shock and surprise. Through the little "O" mouths of these last, he got a clear view of the pieces of Mrs. Edna Chalmers inside. The foot-stool sized pumpkin that held her head was of the "surprised" variety. A big, wooden handled meat fork was jammed savagely into the side.

Inside each gourd was a chintzy, flickering LED light. Blue, purple and red light glittered off the pools of blood that were overflowing the hollow mouths of the pumpkins. It was the only light there was in the place.

"Quite the spectacle, huh?" asked Blackwood, coming around the sign that gave the entire scene a hint of black comedy:

Don't miss our Famous Punkin' Chunkin!

"Yeah," agreed Al. "Anything in the house?"

Blackwood nodded. "Yeah. There are signs of a struggle in the kitchen. Lots of blood in the living room. That's probably where it happened." He looked over at the patrol car. "Where's the kid that called it in?"

"They took him home. He was scared shitless."

"That we'd charge him with trespassing?"

Al stared at John for a moment. "No, John. By the thirty-one pieces of farmer's wife that are oozing onto the ground."

"Oh," said Blackwood. "Right."

John Blackwood was a brilliant investigator and could deduce huge amounts of detail from the tiniest clue—but his social skills were strongly lacking. Milton thought that it was precisely this low degree of empathy that made John so effective when investigating the sociopathic crimes they'd built their reputation on. Mostly, though, it drove Al crazy.

Running down the line of pumpkins with his flashlight, Blackwood asked, "All the pieces here?"

"Yeah," said Al, "From what I can see. You ready for the old man?"

"He's still here?" Blackwood turned to face his partner.

"Yeah. Out in the barn." replied Milton. "The meds did their best, but he got away on them.

"All right," said Blackwood. "Let's see what we can get from the body before they take him away."

"Fair enough," said Milton. "Damned flickering is giving me a headache anyway."

They walked toward the barn, following Blackwood's flashlight beam.

"You're quiet tonight." said John.

"Just thinking," replied Milton. "I told the uniform not to get freaked by the details. It's murder. Murder happens every day."

Blackwood stopped. "It doesn't though, Al. Not like *this*." He looked back at the pumpkins. "For a man to go to such lengths—this was building up for a long while. This wasn't a momentary loss of control."

Inside the barn, which had been turned into a makeshift apartment, there was a ratty looking yellow sofa, a small television, and three large garbage bags. The smell of pumpkin was overpowering.

Three battery powered lanterns created a harsh circle of white light near the sofa. Mike Thurgis, an EMT who had been on scene with John and Al more than once, waved them over.

"It was thirty seconds too long," said Mike. "Me and Rashid had him back for a second, but the damage was done. We're waiting on the ME to come and call the time."

Al looked past Mike to the body on the floor. "He say anything before he went?"

Mike went pale.

"Yeah," he said. "Matter of fact, he did."

Blackwood had his pad out. "Okay—what did you get?"

"He said *Peter Peter*. Twice—just like that—*Peter Peter*." Turning around, the EMT looked in the stall too. "Then he started *laughing*. That was the end of it. He choked on his own blood, and we couldn't get him back."

Al moved around the others and crouched by the body. The man was wire-thin, but his limbs were ropy with sun-hardened muscle. Blood was drying in dark splotches across his swollen, blue-tinged face.

"What are these blood spots here?" he asked Mike.

"I'm not a dick," said Mike. "They're puncture wounds, but you tell me what it means."

The medic lifted the farmer's shirt. Milton exhaled sharply. The man's chest was covered in hundreds of tiny circular scars. Blood was congealing over two of these.

"The meat fork," said Blackwood.

"Yeah." Al agreed. "Seems like Edna'd been poking at her hubby for quite a while, too. Old Peter here probably just had enough."

Blackwood burst out laughing.

"What? What is it, John?" Al stood up.

"You may be a sick bastard, but you've got a sense of humour," said Blackwood, bending down to address the corpse. He looked over at Milton.

"Think about it, Al. *All* of it."

Al did. After a moment, he shook his head, unable to suppress his own uncomfortable grin. "Sick fuck," he muttered.

"What the hell are you guys talking about?" asked Mike.

Blackwood nudged the body with his toe. "All we have to do is write this one up. Think Hollis would appreciate the short version?"

Milton shook his head. "No."

Mike started to object again; Al held up a hand. "It's like this, Mike:

"Peter Peter, pumpkin eater,
Had a wife but couldn't keep her,
He put her in a pumpkin shell…"

Blackwood finished,

"And there he kept her, very well."

NEWSPAPER HAT

On Wednesday night, I made a friend.
She followed me, and we played pretend.

She liked my newspaper hat.

We ascended to my moonlit home.
My tiny place where I live alone.

And make my newspaper hats.

She yelled when she met my little cat,
So shrivelled and quiet on his mat.

I took off my newspaper hat.

Her screaming filled the indigo night.
Blood spattered all over my little light.

And ruined my newspaper hat.

KITTENS FOR SALE

Thomas was thirteen minutes into his lunch hour when he heard the sound. Per usual, he'd taken his brisk walk around the block, finishing back in front of the sandwich shop just beside Barker and Strob's executive office, where he worked as a ruthlessly efficient data clerk.

He was replaying Amanda's voicemail again, dissecting her tone to see where, exactly, he'd gone wrong. Currently, he was staring at the calendar on his phone, trying to remember if it had something to do with forgetting… her… oh God… birthday.

He had the door to "Sub Town" halfway open when he heard the mewling in the alley just a few feet away.

The cardboard sign read "KITT3NS 4 Sale". It was hand-lettered in marker and propped up against a large cardboard box. The seller was about eight years old and was currently sitting against the dusty redbrick of his workplace.

"Want to buy a kitty, mister?" She got to her feet and raised her head of dirty blonde curls.

As John Strob often remarked during his weekly staff meetings, "Timing is everything." Thomas looked at the box and saw a way out of his predicament. He could hear Amanda's squeals of rapture even now.

"That depends, sweetie, how much are they?" Thomas had his hand on his wallet. He hoped sincerely that he'd be buying a cat in the next few minutes, not being mugged from behind by this urchin's accomplice.

"I don't know how much mister. What do you think they're worth?" The girl was looking directly at him now, with eyes the colour of lake water. There was a musty, fungal odour coming from her, like wet laundry that had been left too long. He wondered if she was homeless. Still, no reason he couldn't still make a good deal, " How does ten dollars sound?"

The girl looked back at the box, "I guess that would be okay. Only…"

Thomas paused. There was always a catch, "Only what?"

"Only I don't want you to have one if you're not going to take good care of it. They're sad right now, 'cause they weren't treated nice before." She tucked a strand of wet hair that had been hanging in her eyes behind her ear. (It wasn't wet before, was it? Thomas was puzzled.) In response to her attention, the mewling coming from the box increased.

"I don't understand… sorry, what's your name?" Thomas was feeling less and less at ease.

"My friends call me Jenny, but my name's really Jennifer." She was petting her brood now. Purring like an idling motorboat drifted out of the box.

"Jenny, I don't understand what you mean," Thomas was officially unsettled, "Aren't these your cats? Where did you get them?"

"I found them when I woke up this morning. They were lost, so I wanted to get them a good home. Hi kitty-kitty." Jenny's voice was slightly different, like she was speaking with a mouthful of something. Thomas's phone buzzed. It would be Amanda, trying to give him one last chance to hang himself. He made his decision.

"Right, Jenny. Here's ten bucks. I'd love to buy a kitten." He moved to the box as he was speaking, wanting to pick up the damned cat and get on with his life as soon as possible.

Upon reaching the carton, he went to his knees and vomited. Inside the box had been an open garbage bag, filled with soggy, furry, bloated corpses, tiny holes gaping up at him where fish had eaten the eyes. The mewling was louder than ever.

"They were lost, mister. Nobody wanted them. Just like nobody wanted me. I guess you don't want us either." The voice burbled down at him, all traces of humanity gone, and yet the sense of deep sadness was unmistakable.

Thomas couldn't make himself look up, for fear her face would be like those of the kittens, a ruined and wet mess where a precocious child used to be. The smell overwhelmed him then, a scent of waterlogged rot and ruined meat that made him heave once more.

As he remained crouched over, he saw Jenny walking away down the alley, box in arms, singing a lullaby to her kittens, bleach-white legs trailing seaweed behind them.

The kittens were purring again.

THE MOUSTACHE

"Honey, come look at this." Kelly had been staring into the mirror for over five minutes. Nothing had changed.

Marnie stepped just inside the bathroom door. She was in the middle of fastening her pale blue bra, the new one. Normally, even after eight years together, this was an operation that never failed to draw his eye. Today, he hardly noticed.

"Kel, what are you doing?" Marnie asked. "You're going to be late."

"Just come look for a second," Kelly repeated.

With a resigned sigh, that wasn't all the way exasperated—yet—Marnie walked down the short corridor of the bathroom to join him at the mirror. The enormous shower had been a major selling point when they'd bought this house, but Kelly had always found it a little peculiar to have such a narrow pathway inside a room. Outside, the Gunnarson's dog was raising holy hell. The Schnauzer's constant yelping had never endeared it to Kelly. Today, it was like a screwdriver in his ear, adding pain to an already surreal situation.

"All right," said Marnie, coming to stand beside him. "What is it?"

"Look in the mirror," said Kelly. "What do you see?"

Marnie glanced at the mirror.

"A whitehead. Right next to your nose. Gross." She looked back at him. "Are you going to be much longer? I need to get ready, too."

"No," he said. "Just another two minutes, and I'll be out." His voice sounded far away to him. Kelly watched Marnie leave, and then turned back to his reflection. It was the same face that had been looking back at him for years, with one exception—he had never,

ever, worn a moustache before. The Kelly in the mirror was staring back at him, with the same look of bewilderment that he now felt, except that it was doing so over a full, black handlebar moustache. For the third time, Kelly ran fingers across his upper lip. It was stubbly, but there was certainly no sign of the impressive bristles he saw in the mirror. Aware that Marnie was waiting, Kelly ran the hot water again, lathered up quickly with Gillette, and shaved.

In the mirror, Moustache Kelly did everything he did, at the exact same time, with an identical razor. The difference was that the moustache was covered in shaving foam and looked like a snow-covered hedge. Kelly shaved his lip twice, pressing as hard as he dared. Moustache Kelly followed his movements but moved the razor up and down in front of the moustache. Finishing up, Kelly washed his face with hot water and rubbed on his aftershave balm. His double did the same, and when the two Kellys were finished, the moustache was as full as ever, and twice as glossy.

Kelly tried not to look at the mirror anymore. He slapped on his deodorant and left the bathroom. In the bedroom, he stopped dead in front of Marnie's vanity mirror. The moustache was gone. Where it had been, he saw two tiny cuts that were welling blood—which was what he should have been seeing in the bathroom.

"What the hell is with you today?" asked Marnie, pushing past him on the way to the bathroom. "You're acting funny."

"No. I'm... fine," said Kelly, "I guess." He took a tissue from the box on the vanity and blotted the blood on his lip. "I must have slept badly, or something," he added.

Marnie didn't hear. She was already in the bathroom.

A thought suddenly occurred to him, and he poked his head around the corner of the bathroom door. Would she have a moustache? Now that she was alone in front of the mirror? It was hard to make out her reflection from the bedroom, but he saw himself reflected small in the distance. Part of his face looked too dark. He turned away.

This is nuts, he thought, and turned his full attention to getting dressed and out the door.

By the time he was kissing Marnie goodbye, he was starting to be convinced that he'd been half-asleep, and the moustache was a lingering part of a very peculiar dream.

"Remember," said Marnie, "dinner with my uncle tonight."

Kelly groaned. Earl Walters was an obnoxious prick who'd never let a single opportunity to pick on Kelly slip away. Whether it was his "girl's name", or his being a fan of the Red Wings, Earl was never at a loss for an asinine remark.

"I'll see you there," said Kelly. "But we're not staying long, right?"

Marnie hugged him. "Right." She straightened his tie. "Talk to you later on?"

"Yeah," he said. "I'll call you around lunchtime."

"Feel better, honey."

"I hope so."

***

All that day, Kelly was obsessed with mirrors. Everywhere he went, if there was so much as a reflective surface, he had to take a look. There was no moustache on his face. Brad Broadbent, who worked in the adjacent office, had made a few smart-ass remarks about Kelly "getting vain in his old age," but he'd laughed it off, at the same time trying to sneak a glimpse of his upper lip in Broadbent's silver tie clip.

When Kelly got back to his desk, Carla was waiting for him. Kelly swallowed hard. Carla wasn't bad to work for. Kelly got along very well with her, but she didn't come into someone's office unless she had business to discuss.

Now, she was standing in front of his desk, scrolling the screen on her Blackberry. She looked up as he entered.

"Kelly," she said. "How are you feeling?"

He tried to resist touching his upper lip. It itched where he'd cut it, but more than that, the desire to see if the moustache was there was almost too much to bear.

"I'm fine," he managed, aware that he'd taken far too long to answer.

"You don't seem yourself today. Are you sure?" She was looking him in the eye now. Her dark brown eyes had an intensity that was hard to meet, and it demanded the truth.

"No," he said. "I'm not feeling that great, now that you mention it." *And I feel like I have a giant black moustache on my face. Do you see it?* he finished to himself. His lip was almost twitching now with weird, phantom sensations.

Carla nodded, "Do you have any meetings this afternoon?"

Kelly thought for a second, and not to be thinking about his face for a moment felt wonderful. After mentally fast forwarding through his afternoon he said, "No. I'm all clear."

"Why don't you head home then," said Carla. "Get some rest. Come back tomorrow when you're feeling better."

As soon as she left, Kelly let out the breath he'd been holding in. He didn't know what was happening to him, but he was glad he wouldn't have to fake his way through the rest of the day. It took an effort, but he managed to get out the door without touching his face again.

***

In the car, on his way home, Kelly ignored the angry honks of other drivers as he swerved in and out of his lane. He couldn't take his eyes off the rearview mirror. The irritated, tingly feeling that had started at the office was getting worse, but the mirror only showed the same bare face that he'd gone to bed with last night.

As he neared his street, he remembered dinner with Earl, and checked the clock. It was only three. *Plenty of time to check in at home first.* Plenty of time to check the bathroom mirror, he thought.

He pulled into the driveway and got out, but before he could make it inside, Janice Gunnarson came running over from her front yard.

She was talking before she reached him. "Kelly? Kelly, I'm glad you're home. Scotty's missing."

It took a moment to realize she was talking about the dog.

Unsure what response she was looking for, he said, "Oh?"

"You didn't see him today, did you?" There was panic in her voice.

Maybe if you'd keep the little bark-machine inside now and then, you wouldn't have lost him, thought Kelly. Instead, he said "Sorry, Janice. I left the house at seven-thirty, and he was still barking."

"But what about earlier?" she pressed. "Weren't you at home a few hours ago? Working in your yard? Didn't you see him then?"

Kelly's stomach turned over, and he felt the blood drain from his face.

Janice took no notice of the effect she'd had. "Please. Could you help me look for him?" She seemed on the verge of tears. Kelly could relate. The itch on his upper lip was driving him crazy.

"I'm… I'm sorry Janice. I've been at work all morning, and I came home to lie down." He started to walk into the house. It seemed vitally important that he get inside as soon as possible.

"But…" she started after him.

It was enough. He stopped and spun around. "I feel like shit, Janice," he snapped. "I'm going to go lie down. If I see anything later, you'll be the first to know. All right?"

Janice didn't answer. She stood where she was for a moment. Fat tears rolled down her cheeks. Finally, she turned and started walking awkwardly up the sidewalk, shouting the dog's name in a thick, choked voice. Kelly didn't wait to see if she was coming back. He ran up the steps and let himself in.

Without taking off his shoes or jacket, he sprinted upstairs. Once there, however, he hesitated by the bedroom light switch. He wanted to see, but at the same time, he was terrified of what it would mean if the moustache was back.

Weren't you at home a few hours ago?

A small breeze puffed through the window next to his side of the bed. The window looked out on the backyard. Kelly went to the window and closed it. From here, he could see the weedy, rocky patch in the backyard that he'd had on his to-do list to clean up and plant since spring. The earth looked darker than normal. It was freshly turned. His long-handled spade was jammed into the dirt and leaning toward the house.

The itching on his upper lip returned without warning. It felt like someone had touched the skin with a lit match. His fingers went back across his lip. There was still nothing there.

Kelly charged to the bathroom door, needing to see. He stopped. From here, he could see the reflection of the door behind him. The mirror made the walkway seem twice as long, making it look like his "other" self was a world away. Where did that doorway go? He was convinced now that it didn't go into his own bedroom. But *where* then? He flicked the light on and walked quickly toward the mirror— and his own moustachioed image.

Kelly gasped. Moustache Kelly gasped—but was there a malicious glint in the other's eye? How could that be? Kelly squeezed his right eye shut. His reflection dutifully closed its left at the same time, but now it looked like he was winking. He touched his lip again, needing reassurance.

He froze. His reflection's hands were covered in dirt.

Kelly touched the glass with his relatively clean hands. He saw the deep lines of his own palm full of garden earth. It was under the other's nails as well. Taking the soap from its dish, he turned on the water and scrubbed his hands. Moustache Kelly did the same. When he was done, the sink on his side was clean, with little bubbles of foam popping in the drain. On the other side of the mirror, nothing had changed. His other's hands were still caked with soil and something else—something red. (Have you seen Scottie?)

A burst of electric chimes split the silence. Kelly jumped. His reflection, for once, looked exactly as shocked as he did. He pulled out his Blackberry and saw the "New Message" indicator. Thumbing over it, he saw the note from "Marnie (Cell)"

Remember. Dinner @ Earl's place. Try to be on time.

He made the screen go off and jammed it back in his pocket. Great. The last thing he needed right now was to...

Oh no, he thought. The phone sat, silent and heavy in his hand. What if he knows? His eyes flicked back to the mirror. Did he see the hint of a smile on his double's face? It was hard to tell with the damned moustache in the way. Suddenly, there didn't seem to be a right thing to do. If he left the room, he'd set the other free. On the other hand, he couldn't stay in the bathroom forever. The eyes in the mirror were his own, but the reflection seemed not to show any of what he was feeling. He touched his face.

Watching his hand touch that god-awful strip of hair was the final straw. He couldn't look at it anymore. Shoving his phone into his pocket, Kelly practically ran from the room, stumbled down the stairs, and got in his car.

***

Traffic was a mess. From the office, Earl's place was twenty minutes away. From home, and in rush-hour, it would likely take an hour to get there. He'd be late, and Earl would get snarky.

After forty minutes of bumper to bumper driving on Wallace Ave., Kelly was waiting at a red light when his phone went off again. He picked up, and for a moment, could only hear someone crying.

"Hello?" he said. The display said "Marnie (Cell)". His breath caught in his throat. "Marn?" he managed. "What is it?"

"E-Earl," she said, finally. "His heart."

"What happened?" he asked. But he knew what it must be.

"They're not sure," she said. "He's still in emerg. Come quickly, okay? It's St. Paul's—on Pinewood."

"All right," he replied, and hung up. Kelly flipped his indicator from left to right, and drove to the hospital with his heart pounding, and his eyes fixed on the rear-view mirror.

***

Thirty minutes later, he met Marnie in the hallway of the Emergency Ward. Her eyes were puffy and red from crying. They hugged in silence for awhile.

Speaking into his chest, Marnie told him that she'd left work early, and headed to Earl's to help finish up dinner. When she arrived, she'd found paramedics just closing up the ambulance.

Kelly shuddered. I was outside talking to Janice by then. What had his "other" been doing? He had a sudden mental image of Moustache Kelly, hands still streaked with dirt and blood from the yard work, going into Earl's house. He shuddered involuntarily, and wiped his hands on his jeans, trying to get rid of dirt that wasn't there.

"It's all right," Marnie said, drawing back a bit to look him in the eye. "He's going to come through…" she broke off her last words, and gasped. "What have you been doing to your face, Kel?"

Oh God, he thought, the moustache! He reached up and stroked his lip again. For the first time that day, he was aware of pain when he did so. His skin felt hot to the touch, and he had to take his hand away.

"I had an itch," he said, knowing how lame it sounded. "I guess I kept scratching at it without thinking."

"You should get someone here to look at it," Marnie said. "I think it's getting infected." She grabbed his chin lightly and turned his head slightly back and forth. "How could you not notice? It's raw."

"Never mind that," said Kelly, taking her hand off his face, and holding it. "It'll be okay. How's Earl?"

"Okay for the moment. They won't let me see him yet, but it looks like he's out of danger."

Asking about her uncle seemed to jar Marnie back to thinking about other things. It was a small relief. More than anything right now, Kelly wanted to find a mirror. How could he have chaffed himself so thoroughly without noticing?

The answer was simple. He hadn't been looking at his lip, not really. Instead, he'd been looking for something that refused to show itself- except in the mirror in their en suite, that was.

"You should put something on that, at least," said Marnie. "To keep you from touching it until you can get it looked at." Her voice was getting stronger—she was going into her "take charge" mode. Kelly didn't argue; it was easier to deal with a bossy Marnie than a crying, helpless one. She stopped a passing nurse.

"Excuse me," said Marnie. "Could you get a bandage for my husband? He hurt his lip, but we're waiting to find out about my uncle."

The nurse looked at Kelly, and winced. "I don't think you want to put anything on that until a doctor's seen it."

"I keep touching it," said Kelly. "I don't mean to, but I do, and it's making it worse. Do you have something?" He had to force his hand back to his side even now. "I'm going to ask to get seen at the desk here—but how high a priority am I going to be with all these other people waiting?" It was true. The waiting room was crowded with people coughing, people sneezing, and people grabbing body parts and wincing every time someone in scrubs walked by.

"Fair enough," said the nurse. "I'm in Paeds, though—so your choices..." she dug in the pocket of her tunic, "are Scooby Doo, or Spiderman."

Kelly grinned self-consciously. Either way, he was going to look like an idiot. He took a black Spiderman bandage, with a pattern of red webs printed on top. The nurse, who was prettier than Kelly would have preferred, with Marnie standing right next to him, helped put the strip on his face. He thanked her, and she left. When he turned to face Marnie, she giggled.

"What?" he asked. "I look stupid, don't I?"

"You have a moustache," she said, laughing again. "It's cute."

"Cute" was the last thing that Kelly felt. Light-headed, nauseous and terrified were more apt descriptions at the moment. He ran his fingers over the smooth surface of the bandage. The pressure made him wince.

"Stop that," said Marnie. "That's what got you in trouble in the first place."

They waited in the Emergency Waiting room for another hour before another nurse came to talk to them. She wasn't unfriendly, but she didn't waste time with small talk, either. Earl was awake and had been moved to a bed in the Emergency Ward. It looked, for the moment, that he'd suffered an attack of angina, rather than a full-on heart attack. He was in pain but seemed to be through the worst of it. Marnie and Kelly could visit for a moment, but the hospital was going to be moving him to a room for overnight observation.

"Do you want to go in?" asked Marnie.

"I'm not sure," said Kelly. "Earl probably doesn't want to see me."

"Come with me," Marnie insisted.

"I'm not sure, Marn," said Kelly. He really didn't want to see Earl right now. His hands still felt filthy, which was ridiculous. If his other had done something awful to Scottie, what the hell had he been up to with Earl?

"Kelly, I need you with me," said Marnie.

"What if they call me? I'd hate to have to start waiting all over again," he replied. It was lame, but it was also all he could think of.

"Hang on," the nurse interjected. She moved behind the desk and checked a stack of charts. "You're not going anywhere for awhile."

"But…" Kelly started to say. The nurse cut him off.

"Don't worry," she said. "I'll come find you if your name comes up."

Kelly was out of excuses, and Marnie took him by the arm as they followed the nurse through a set of double doors, and into a large area with a line of curtained-off rooms.

"Maybe we should let him sleep," said Kelly.

"We'll just poke our heads in for a second," she insisted.

Kelly sighed. Marnie's face was set in an all too familiar expression that dared him to test her will.

They went in.

Earl was wearing a pale green mask over his face. It fogged with his deep, regular breaths. A machine beside the bed had wires attached that lead beneath the sheet to his chest.

There were no signs of a physical fight from what Kelly could see of Earl's face and arms. That was good. What had his double done? He blinked, and suddenly, an image flashed behind his eyes. He saw himself—or rather, his Moustachioed other standing in front of Earl's door. That Kelly was slamming a golf club against the door. There was no sound, but the double's mouth was open, as if he was screaming something.

Marnie went to Earl's side. Kelly held her back.

"Let him rest," he said, trying to keep his voice steady. His heart was beating at a suicidal pace in his ears. "There'll be lots of time to visit when he goes upstairs."

Suddenly, the beeping from the heart monitor sped up. Kelly looked back. Earl's eyes were bugging out.

"Y... Y... Yo..." he was trying to talk. Spittle flew from his liver-coloured lips. The beeping grew faster. It was joined by a louder, steady alarm that was likely summoning the doctors.

As quick as he could, Kelly left the room. On the way out, he had to stand aside to let two nurses in patterned scrubs rush by him. Marnie followed him out into the hall, looking stricken.

"What was that about, Kelly? What's going on?"

"I don't know," he said.

The beeping from the heart monitor started to slow, and the alarm shut off. Kelly felt like his own heart was beating fast enough to burst.

He sat with Marnie until the nurse returned to tell them that Earl had been stabilized again, but that they wouldn't be allowed to see him again until the following day. As they went back into the Emergency Waiting room, the triage nurse called his name. Without thinking about it, he touched his lip again, and winced. It hurt. Great, he thought. One more thing to worry about.

✱✱✱

"Well," said the doctor, who looked five years younger than Kelly, "I don't think you're going to be surprised at what I'm going to tell you to do."

"Stop touching it?" Kelly offered, with an edge of sarcasm in his voice. He wasn't in the mood for light-hearted bedside manner. "That's what I waited two hours to hear?"

"You can't shave, either," said the doctor, his voice becoming more clinical. *Fine*, his expression seemed to say, *be an asshole*.

The doctor scrawled something on a prescription pad.

"I'm prescribing a cortisone cream to help with the inflammation. Use this cream three times a day, for about ten days. If it's not starting to get better after two days or so, go see your family doctor, alright?"

"Got it." said Kelly. He tried to muster real sincerity. If he ever ended up in this emergency room again, he didn't want this doctor to remember him as a prick.

As the doctor was leaving, Kelly said, "Thanks, doctor. Really."

The doctor turned back and smiled, "You're welcome." His expression suddenly changed, "But seriously, Kelly—stop touching it."

Kelly had no response to that. He realized, to his horror, that he had been rubbing his face again. His fingers came away slick. A blister had popped, and he could feel fluid trickling into the corner of his mouth. There was a tiny sink in the corner of the examination room, and he spat into it. His thoughts were racing. It seemed impossible that only this morning, everything had been perfectly normal, until he'd walked into the bathroom. Now, he'd developed an unconscious tic that was destroying his face—and worse—there was no telling what that "other" Kelly was doing right now. That he was even thinking in those terms made his head spin. Maybe he was going crazy. He hoped so. It would make things so much easier to understand.

***

The first time Kelly applied the medicated salve to his lip, it had felt like he'd poured rubbing alcohol into an open wound—then lit it on fire. After the fourth application, the pain seemed to lessen. Marnie had been ruthless in stopping him from touching his face, though she still thought the reason for his self-injury was a phantom itch. That was cause enough for concern, but how much worse would it have been, Kelly thought, if he insisted on telling her that he was constantly checking to see if he had a moustache—which, under doctor's orders, he was now growing.

Besides taking care of his skin, Kelly did his best to keep his anger in check. It was tough though, as Broadbent could provoke a priest to violence with his constant, mindless, ignorant banter. How sweet it would be, Kelly thought sometimes, to know that his Moustachioed "other" might find Broadbent one night and give him a little scare. Kelly pushed these types of dreams away. Things had gotten way too close, and way too creepy, with Earl. There was no way he'd get that lucky again.

A week later, his "real" moustache was growing in nicely. He was almost through with the salve, which was a relief, as it was starting to be a pain to comb through the tiny hairs to keep it from looking matted. Originally, Marnie had given him funny looks when he walked in the house at the end of the day. It was just so odd, she said, seeing him with a moustache. Soon though, and to their mutual surprise, she found that she liked it. Though she never would have thought to suggest it, she'd said, it gave him an air of mystery that was "a bit of a turn-on."

Kelly was feeling better mentally, too. Having made a drastic change to his appearance seemed to have made a dramatic change to his personality. He was more assertive at work, and several times put Broadbent in his place, with exactly the right word at exactly the right time. Even his "other" had ceased to bother him. As the hair on his face grew, Kelly noticed, with some amusement, that the other's moustache was getting shorter, and thinner. It didn't bother him to stay in the bathroom anymore; the second Kelly seemed almost impotent now.

Earl recovered, and to Kelly's relief, he didn't remember anything about the incident that had put him in the hospital. However, his demeanour toward his niece's husband had grown perceptibly more respectful—even a little fearful at times. Kelly didn't mind.

***

One morning, about eight weeks after the entire business had begun, Kelly was checking his hair in Marnie's vanity mirror, and it struck him that his facial hair was now an exact match to the moustache he'd seen that had started the whole crazy business. Soft, trimmed black whiskers flowed across his upper lip, and curled down slightly at the edge of his mouth before twisting back up with a natural flourish. This was the style that felt right. With this realization, though, came a curious impulse to go check the ensuite mirror, to see what his "other" was doing.

At the doorway, Kelly flicked on the light. A thought dawned in his mind, and he knew—without a doubt—what he was about to see. He kept his eye on the reflection as he walked in.

Moustache Kelly was no more. The figure in the mirror was him, but his face was totally bare. The expression in the other's eyes was something else. In the reflection, the other's eyes were wide, staring desperately at the world on this side of the glass. Kelly-in-the-real-world put his hand up to the glass. The double's hand came up with his. It was shaking. Suddenly, all pretence of reflection broke down, and the clean-faced image of Kelly began beating its fists in soundless fury on the other side of the glass. Beneath his full, black moustache, Kelly smiled.

THE SINS OF THE PAST

Spencer stared at the screen. He looked away, and then back. Nothing had changed. He felt as if he'd swallowed a rubber ball. It was all that was left from his time as an employee of Leonard Dallas. He'd kept the thirteen dollars to remind himself that no amount of money was worth sacrificing his principles for… again. Today, however, the total read $1,013.

✳✳✳

After a string of disastrous results betting on horses, basketball, and football, he'd owed the bookie forty thousand dollars. Seeing that there was no way he was going to be able to pay and, loathe to waste the resources of a financial wizard, a deal had been struck. Spencer had laundered money for the organization for five months, using every loophole and trick at his disposal to not only get the funds clean, but to grow them substantially on the way. At no time, however, did he forget that he was the last link in the chain of money, and the first to go if the cops started sniffing around.

At the end of five months, Leonard called him into the office, and released him from his "contract." The man was huge. At six-foot-six (at least) he was like a transport truck wrapped up in Armani. He'd offered to keep Spencer on the payroll, having liked the way he kept his books clean and his mouth shut, but Spencer had read enough crime novels to know that if you're ever offered a way out, you take it. Even then, the last ten years had passed with Spencer constantly waiting for the other shoe to drop.

***

Today it had, to the tune of one thousand dollars. Spencer reached for his coffee, and instead found himself groping the stamp-pad he'd left open.

"Shit." Momentarily distracted with pulling handfuls of tissue out of the box, and trying to wipe his fingers off, the phone had gotten to its third ring by the time he noticed. The name on the display was "Ewing Investments." Dallas. It was a terrible joke, but no one dared tell Leonard that. With trembling hands, Spencer snatched up the receiver, and bought himself a moment to prepare by spouting the script, "Good Morning, you've reached Wellington Investments, this is Spencer Davis speaking, how may I help you today?" Better. It was the mental equivalent of taking a deep breath, which he did next.

"Spence. How's things?"

He winced at the uncomfortable familiarity, and shifted the now partially blue telephone under his shoulder, "Mr. Dallas?"

The voice on the other end came back brightly, "No, this is Gerard. You remember us, though. I'm deeply touched. As you can see, we haven't forgotten about you either."

Spencer forced himself to take a moment, then sucked back half the steaming cup of coffee in one gulp. He grimaced at the heat. Gerard was not in a waiting mood it seemed. "Spence? Still there?"

He spluttered around the dregs of his coffee, "Yes… I mean yes, sir, I'm here. I had a tickle in my throat and didn't want to cough into the phone."

"Fine. So, tell me, did you take a look at your bank records?"

Spencer surprised himself. Now that the moment he'd been quietly dreading for a decade was here, he found that he was remarkably calm. "I did. It was a surprise."

"It wasn't that hard finding your new information, Spence. We wanted to re-introduce ourselves, as it were, with a gift. Something to show that what we're proposing is at heart, mutually beneficial."

"And what's that?"

"I'm in a car downstairs. Come down, and we'll talk about it." The connection ended. It hadn't been a request.

Minutes later, Spencer was in the back of a limousine, facing the man himself. The heavy black car was leaning just perceptibly to the side which held the juggernaut. Dallas was currently smiling at him and sipping from a glass of scotch.

"Let me get right to the point, Spencer. You don't like me. That's okay. Very few people do. It won't stop me from making you an offer. I need you to do some more work for us. One job."

It was exactly as he'd feared. He had to at least put up the pretence of refusal, though the bulge in Gerard's suit coat indicated his options were far more restricted than they seemed. "Mr. Dallas, I really appreciate it, but I came so close to losing my license last time, I really couldn't…"

"Stop right there, Spencer. You can rest assured you won't be going near our books this time."

Before the banker could even breathe his sigh of relief, however, the big man continued, "No, no, just a quick and easy homicide."

Spencer fainted.

***

His face stung as he came awake. Gerard had been slapping him. Hard. He held up his hand, "Stop. Please."

With the exception of the level of booze in Dallas' glass, nothing else had changed. The boss continued.

"There now Spencer. We lost you for a minute there. I see this is a big surprise to you, but you have to know we wouldn't be asking you to do this if there were any other way."

The thin young man rubbed his swelling cheek and mumbled, "I can't kill anyone."

In response, he now faced the unblinking eye of Gerard's automatic. "Can't allow you to leave then, Spence. You've heard us use the 'm' word, after all."

It had been made that simple then: take a life or lose his own. When considered like that, Spencer Davis, who had succumbed to the allure of quick money at the track, who had turned to illegal means to repay his losses, who, in short, always took the easy way—the choice was no choice at all.

"Who is it you need… who's the tar… who is it?"

At this, Dallas produced a plain manila envelope, open at one end. He removed a picture and handed it to Spencer. The woman was startlingly beautiful. If you took away all the gaudy jewellery, heavy eye-makeup, and kerchief, she could easily be the celebrity face of some women's beauty product.

"Why her?" Dallas must have thought this was reasonable, because he answered.

"Fair enough Spencer, it's your first time, so hopefully having a purpose will make it easier."

He sat back, and continued, "Rosemary Dugayi. Fortune teller. She has one of those little studios, you know the type, neon hand with an eye in it shining out of a shitty little second floor window? Ms Dugayi not only overheard some of our sensitive business, but she also made a recording. Shame on us for using the adjoining apartment for something so important, but what's done is done. Now, here is where you come in."

Spencer was sipping a Perrier that Gerard had passed over as a low-level peace-offering. He raised his eyebrows, offering no objection. Leonard continued.

"Though I discount entirely any claims the woman may have to supernatural power, I must admit that she has shown an infuriating knack for knowing when any of my men are near—ensuring then that she is not. In short, we can't get close to her."

Gerard pressed a nine-millimetre pistol into his hand. The gun felt heavy and foreign in Spencer's grip. He detested the thing at once. The slender bodyguard watched his reaction and said, "It's loaded. That little switch on the side is called a safety. Move it over before you need to fire. Remember to *squeeze* the trigger. Don't pull it—you're liable to break your finger otherwise."

Spencer gulped, and Dallas went on. "You're going to visit Ms Dugayi as a client. Book a fortune telling. Do this yourself. If we do it, she'll know. Go to your appointment; let her do her thing. Then, when it's time to pay, you take out the gun instead of your wallet, and presto: I'm happy, and you're forty-thousand dollars to the black. That is, if things go right. If you miss this opportunity, we won't get another, and I shall be displeased. I think it goes without saying that you don't want me to be displeased with your performance."

Gerard chimed in, "They'll find your fucking head in the freezer."

Dallas shot the man a look that could melt iron. "Gerard. A little decorum. Bear in mind that we're asking this man to go well outside his comfort zone, and I can see by his expression that he will be doing everything in his power to ensure things go as planned. Right Spencer?"

Spencer nodded, still looking down at the ugly black gun. He had a crazy notion flit through his mind then. What if he just opened fire right now? Took out both these madmen in one go? Sure, he thought, if I can figure out how to get the damned safety off before Gerard blows three holes in my skull. Instead, he just kept nodding.

"Now then, the address is on the back of the photo."

***

It was twenty minutes past eight when Spencer made his way up the musty, yellowed stairway that smelled of age and long-dead cigarettes. The brown metal apartment door was adorned with the same hand and eye symbol he'd seen in the window. There wasn't even a name.

The door was unlocked, but upon opening it, he found himself in a normal looking living room. There was no indication of any business being run out of this place. The result was an uncomfortable moment where he felt like he'd broken in. "Hello?"

"Sit down Mr. Davis."

The voice came from somewhere behind a curtain of black beads. For the life of him, it made Spencer think of that old black and white movie about the Wolfman, "Even a man who is pure in heart and says his prayers by night may become a volf vhen the autumn moon is bright."

When the beads parted, however, he saw that was where any similarity to the old crone in the film left off. She was a petite, smouldering beauty with huge dark eyes, and long auburn hair pulled into a ponytail at the nape of her neck. As she drew near the table, his senses were overwhelmed by her scent, which was feminine and wild at the same time, like making love in the forest.

Still staring, Spencer took a seat. She sat across from him, and bored into him with her black eyes, "Now then, Mr. Davis, let me tell you vhy you vill not shoot me." She smiled then, and he saw that her lips curled oddly at the corners of her mouth, as if the teeth there were just a little bigger than they should be.

Sucker punched, Spencer could do nothing but continue to stare, except now his jaw was hanging open.

In the next forty minutes, Rosemary laid out an intricate spread of tarot cards that all foretold great misfortune, and with far more details than he would have thought possible. It distilled itself to one crystal clear outcome—he was going to die. Whether or not he took this woman's life, Gerard would put a bullet in his head at the earliest opportunity.

His eyes felt dry and red, but no tears came. His survival instincts were all used up, and he was trying to come to terms with his own mortality.

"Mr. Davis... Spencer. Vhat if I told you this outcome could be avoided? Vhat if I could give you the power to reclaim your life? Vhat if I could make you young and strong for always?" She stopped talking then, and just looked at him. There was naked lust in her eyes, and despite his looming demise, Spencer was completely aroused.

Shifting in his seat, he said, "What are you talking about?"

She smiled wider, showing canines that no human should have, "I think you know."

"Will it hurt?"

"A lot."

"After, can we..."

"Yes, I'd like that." Her grin was growing longer still, pulling back and back and back. He could see all her teeth now, but focused instead on her beautiful eyes.

"Alright. I agree."

She pounced, and she was right.

It hurt.

A lot.

***

Several hours later Spencer emerged from beside the storefront, looking much the same as he went in, except now he smelled vaguely of sex and wet dog. He wore a huge grin, and an air of confidence that he'd never had before. The night was alive with the scents of twilight, and the sounds of night birds and insects. His senses were so overwhelmed with minutiae that he didn't notice Gerard stepping out in front of him. The bastard smiled, and pulled the trigger.

Spencer crumpled to the ground, clutching at wounds that burned like fire. Their sting spread quickly throughout his body. He knew what it must mean. Spitting blood, he managed to cough, "Silver bullets? Why? How?"

Gerard sneered, "We heard rumours, and these things are best not left to chance. Besides, it would explain a lot about how she knew we were coming." He checked the clip.

"Eight left for your new girlfriend. Better get on..." he was interrupted by a thick chuffing sound from his victim. "Why in Christ's name are you laughing?"

"Behind you. I… might be dying… but looks like… you… you're out of a job." Spencer's new nose had told him the whole story. It wouldn't be working much longer, but it was working.

Gerard turned in time to see the black limo start rocking violently. There was a thick, bellowing scream and blood sprayed the back window with a splat.

He spit. "Well son of a bitch."

"Psst. Hey Gerry." Spencer's voice, but much rougher coming from behind him made him snap his head around.

"Silver bullets are bullshit."

The werewolf lunged. Strictly speaking, Spencer shouldn't have enjoyed it so much, but this was personal, and he did.

Later, in the woods, he met up with his fortune-teller-sire.

"It verked." She smiled her wolfish grin.

"I guess they never saw it coming."

She rolled her eyes and threw her arms around him. "That's terrible."

"So are we. But I like it."

The moon came from behind a cloud, and the two new lovers went to greet her.

THE CHOIR OF PULCINELLO

"Come closer," the old man cackled drunkenly. "For that pint of ale, I'll tell you a story. Something to keep you company, you might say." He accepted the drink greedily. After a long, messy gulp, he began to speak.

"It was fifteen and ninety, after the big plague. Here in the lonely country, it wasn't so bad, but I was a merchant. Seeing most of your customers die off makes you consider things. I reckoned I'd travel south to Italy, get some sun, and take a few choice items with me.

"Back then I could still sell tinder to the devil, and by the time I reached Milan, I had enough to set up shop in the market square.

"The best business always came when there was a hanging. They called it 'The Executioner's Fair.' I used to know the Italian for that. I can't recall it now. People would come from all over to watch the convicts swing. All us merchants did very well. With the fair would come food, musicians and, of course, the Punch and Judy show.

"This particular show, by 'Professore Dante,' was called 'The Choir of Pulcinello.' You've seen the show before, I'll reckon. Old Punch, or Pulcinello if you like, gets the best of his wife, the law, the devil and the hangman, through trickery and that big stick he carries.

"I went to see the show one afternoon, as I had heard everyone talking about it. He did ten shows a day, which also was unheard of, so nearly everyone had seen it. It also meant that Dante was the last to leave every day.

"The show was like nothing I'd ever seen. Up to ten puppets at a time came on. Angels sang in choral harmony as they took Pulch's victims up to heaven. Chaos reigned in court as puppets argued over one another. There was no way this could all come from one man.

"My curiosity got the best of me. That night, I waited, concealed, and followed the Professore as he left. He was a stooped, twisted man, and wore a cloak that obscured his features. I watched as he walked towards the flyspecked corpses that had hung that day. He cut them down, put them on his handcart, and continued down an alley. I had no choice but to follow.

"It was then that I heard the chewing sounds.

"As I made my way down the narrow, yellowed street, I saw the Professore's discarded cloak and shirt. Dread filled me as I rounded the final turn, and beheld insanity.

"The creature was fish belly white, and where I'd seen a hump was, in reality, a muscled clump of tentacles, all engaged on ripping chunks of flesh from the dead. I gasped, and he turned, exposing six gaping mouths erupting from his chest, each lined with needle teeth. All were currently being fed chunks of meat by the flailing arms. I noticed his muddy brown eyes boring into me, and the total absence of a mouth on his face.

"'YOU SHOULD NOT BE HERE.' A cacophony of voices growled. The effect was dizzying. His appendages stiffened then, and the mouths began to hiss, 'Nottt to seee and live!' His eyes rolled back to the whites, and he took a halting step toward me.

"I ran then, as fast as possible back to my lodging, packed what I could carry, and fled for Europe. Hell, it seemed, was truthfully at my heels.

"Not three years later came the Great Plague of Milan, and I prayed that the 'Professore' met his end. But I fear every day that the Corpse-Eater will come looking for me, wanting to silence the only witness to his secret. Except now you know, too."

The traveller motioned for more ale, and put coin on the table. The old man thanked him, and shortly after slumped into a besotted sleep in his chair by the fire. The silent man went upstairs to his room and began to unpack his puppets.

GAME NIGHT

1

We only meet on Friday the 13th. Sometimes this is three times a year, sometimes it's only once, but we always make it back to the tool shed. No one ever skips, and no one is ever late. For six hours, every Friday the thirteenth, we decide the fate of the world. *Mostly. Partly. Sort of.*

My daily life is much like yours. I wake up, I eat something, and I go to work. The only difference is, I'm not showing off by *breathing* the whole time.

Oh, I know what you're thinking, "ghosts don't sleep." When's the last time you asked one? Thought so. Anyway, I eat too, so there's another of your little theories gone. My favourite meal is breakfast. That's when you guys are at your tastiest. Quit worrying, I don't eat *flesh*, it gives me gas. Ever seen a ghost fart? We whip through the room at the speed of light and you guys think something's gone off in the fridge.

No, what I eat is memories. They hang off of you, you know. Your thoughts are part of your soul, and *everyone* knows that your soul is bigger than your body, so I just pick off one or two short-term memories and fill my belly. Mostly I grab the easy stuff, like where you put your car keys, the reminder to thaw out a chicken for dinner, Aunt Kathy's hip surgery, you get the idea. I never touch your long-term memories. They taste like dust and besides, I'm a ghost, not a bastard.

Where the hell was I? You'll have to forgive me. It's tough to keep a single train of thought in your head when you don't really have one. Oh, right, I started to tell you about "the Four." Every

Friday the thirteenth, we meet in a huge commercial tool shed in Sudbury, behind Larry's Lawn Care. It's the most private place we can think of, and the Big Nickel makes us all giddy.

There's me, "Chai Tea", which explains my preference for breakfast. Black Cat and Broken Mirror are a couple, and *fat*—like *huge*... picture a couple of sweaty pink balloons and you'll get the idea. In the same way I feed on memory, they prefer bad luck. Between you and me, I think they're a little too well fed to be getting all their meals "legit" if you catch my drift. I'm especially suspicious of Cat. I saw her downtown last week, sawing through some lady's high heels while she sat on a patio, eating her lunch. This kind of interference is strictly forbidden. Mostly though, it's such piddly stuff that we let it go, which is good, because if the Big Guys got wind, they'd make *our* lives miserable.

That brings me to Miniature Sunflower. Don't let the name fool you. He *is* a bastard. He goes around opening car windows and sunroofs when it rains. He loves chaos and the despair it causes. Every now and then he kills someone, which is above our station, but Sunflower is ambitious, and you can't tell him *anything* when he's out for blood. By the by, don't *ever* call us "ghosts" unless, that is, you want to forget how to tie your shoes, or have every single drive-through coffee you buy explode on your lap. We're touchy on the subject. One time, Sunflower heard a guy who programmed video games laughing about ghosts with his buddies. "The only ghosts are the ones I put on the screen," he'd said. Right about then, a steel truck went by and dropped a 5-tonne coil on his car—with him inside. Sunflower stood there and gave the guy's spirit the finger the whole time he was crossing over. He's all class, is Sunflower.

Okay, now you know everyone. Collectively, the guys in charge used to call us "The Four Minor Gods of Misfortune and Chaos." We're the construction workers of the spirit world, we do what needs to be done, and we're good at it.

This brings us back to Friday the thirteenth. Every time we get together, we play games to find out how much fun we can have at your expense, at least until the next Friday the thirteenth.

I told you about the four of us? There's a fifth—Circle Jim. When we play, it's all of us against him. If he wins, we take it easy, and get terribly hungry. During these times, we go to Vegas.

You wouldn't know this, but the nutritional value of a busted Blackjack hand is about equal to a Twinkie. Sunflower gets particularly crotchety on these trips. After our last trip to Nevada, the

Casinos put in shatterproof windows from the second floor up. So you'll appreciate that when we win against CJ, we binge a little.

On those rare occasions where we win twice in a row, you guys tend to start noticing something's up. Remember the Depression? It was *delicious*.

The crazy thing is that we *don't* win all the time, which, seeing as how it's always four against one, is odd in itself. It just seems to balance out.

The game itself isn't important. We switch it up each time. CJ loves chess, so we almost never play it. He pulls out four boards and turns into Bobby Fischer on us. (Literally. It's as annoying as it sounds.) The worst part is he always plays us to a stalemate. One of the "rules" is that ties go to CJ, because there are four of us, I guess.

The last time we played chess was in the early 90s. We were starting to feel bad about having things so good for so long. The fashions of the 70s, Disco, cocaine? *You're welcome.* Jim won the match and told us to turn the tide and make things a little better. He didn't care how. We got crafty and invented "Dot Coms".

You might wonder to yourself if we had something to do with the events in the last part of 2001. We didn't. I don't like saying their names, but there are spirits out there that are much bigger, and much meaner than any of us combined, and they ride horses. As a matter of fact, we tried to help you out. There were four more planes, and four more planned targets. Only one of the bad guys lost his ticket. Another fell down a flight of stairs and broke his collarbone on the way to the airport. The third got into a cab with a driver that was absolutely clueless, and he missed his flight, and the last was killed when the tires blew out on his car and he went over a cliff. But there are only four of us. I'm sorry.

2

Whoo. Got a little heavy for a minute there. Let's get back to the current Friday the thirteenth. It was poker night. We all crushed out our cigarettes and made our way into the shed. We all smoke, as we dig the irony. Cat and Mirror showed up earlier, and in as good a mood as I've ever seen. Last night's lottery draw was for over two-hundred million. A record number of tickets were sold and by coincidence, there were two winners splitting the prize. One was the wife of a billionaire who played weekly as her "donation to charity," the other was a celebrity who bought the ticket on a whim when he popped into a convenience store for cigarettes.

The tang of sour grapes in the air was palpable, and Broken Mirror was practically swimming in it. I'm guessing Cat was equally jazzed, but she's so goofy most of the time it was hard to tell the difference. They were sitting at the felted card table, wearing matching lime green tracksuits and Elvis sunglasses. And sweating. Watching two morbidly obese spirits mop buckets of sweat from their jiggling jowls is quite a sight. Sunflower strolled in next, flashing me a snaggle-toothed grin as he made his way to the table. He was flipping a large, greasy lag bolt from hand to hand, and then, seeing that he'd caught my attention, tipped me a huge and dirty wink. I raised my eyebrows, and he went back to fiddling with the bolt and humming carnival music. What a jerk.

CJ was the last to arrive. He spun on one cowboy booted heel and slapped the door shut. Then, without missing a beat, he whirled around again to face us, fingers raised in a perfect six-gun simulation. The tassels on his Roy Rogers shirt flipped back and forth in the fluorescent light.

"Whoo-ee, folks!" he shouted. "I feel *good* today! Who wants to play some cards?" His whole persona today seemed designed to grate on our nerves. It was payback, I'm sure. Last time we all got together, and played Monopoly, of all things, I was knocked out early and I stole his iPod. I erased all of his symphonies and operettas, and replaced it with five straight hours of "Baby Shark." So now CJ's gone country. Spirits hate country, or at least *we* all do, CJ excepted. People who play country music in their house almost never misplace their keys. It's a fact.

On the first deal, I got a ten and a seven, not a promising start. I threw in the small blind and waved goodbye to a stack of chips.

Black Cat started giggling. She's got a terrible poker face, worse than me. Her upside is, she can be remarkably stupid. She'll be tee-heeing over a three and a two, and everyone will throw their hand in thinking she's got it made. The downside is, she can be remarkably stupid—she's just as likely to fold with a pair of aces. This happens more often than not. For all the bad luck she causes, she seems to have amazing luck at cards, so she can afford to blow about half of her hands and still come out on top. Broken Mirror, on the other hand, seems to pull winning hands out of his massive behind just enough to keep him in the game. As big as he is, he's really easy-going, and genuinely seems happy just to break even most times.

Jim threw in his big blind with a grin, and the game was on.

3

Ok, each of us gets one hundred chips to start with and each chip is one day. (Don't bother with the math—overlapping is allowed.) The big winner gets to spend the days however they want. We're all really in it for ourselves. It's just worked out that, over the years, CJ balances us off so often that we started working together. When Sunflower's won it all in the past, we've had to remind him of the pact. Sometimes this means spoiling his fun.

Sunflower won big in '93. Two hundred and eighty-six days of accidents, mishaps and bad luck. He decided he wanted to keep them all for himself. This pissed us off to no end. He was planning to run them all together in an attempt to impress the big guys.

As I've mentioned, Sunflower got off on death by misfortune; so he rigged up a faulty pedestrian crosswalk. It would have been genius if it weren't so evil. He set it up so that it would just discharge massive amounts of electricity every so often—it wouldn't kill everyone who pushed the button—it would just happen at random. It was so devious that some people only got a tiny jolt that messed up their heart, and they'd die about twenty minutes later for no apparent reason. The rest of us were horrified. He was breaking a bunch of rules, and we all knew that it wouldn't be good attention he attracted from the Horsemen.

I talked it over with Cat and Mirror, and we brought our plan to Circle Jim. He liked it and let us handle Sunflower our own way.

We staked out the corner, and for the next thirty days, that spot was a terribly unlucky place to visit. They were doing construction on the corner (which is how Sunflower got access to the wiring.) Incidents of falling paint cans went up 400%. The same crew forgot what they were doing and installed a new door in the convenience store that opened out onto the sidewalk. We laughed ourselves hoarse every time someone took one to the face. Lots of broken noses. Zero electrocutions. Other people, about to press the fatal button, suddenly remembered terribly important matters directly back the way they'd come.

First prize, though, went to Cat. That broad is a genius. She solved the whole mess by letting a bee loose in a taxi. The driver ploughed right into the faulty pole, ruining everything.

Sunflower was madder than we'd ever seen. One-to-one, he'd have beaten any of us senseless. Together, though, we were more than a match for him. He backed down that time, and agreed to split up the rest of the days, but he insisted on keeping his share of those. He made good use of them too. Remember that guy who was installing an animated billboard and got flung three city blocks? The lady who was checking her makeup and drove into the lake? And the teenager that fell onto the third rail? Sunflower didn't waste time. I sometimes wonder if he actually was one of us, or something else entirely. The rest of us get up to some pretty mean tricks, but we're never as out and out violent as he was, and we've never killed anyone... on purpose.

4

On the second deal, I got a King and Jack suited in hearts. I thought it might turn out to be something. The betting went around again. I raised. Then Sunflower sprung his surprise.

"Hey Jim, what say we cut the bullshit, okay?"

"Whatcha talkin' about, pard'ner?" CJ kept playing up the western thing, not recognizing that glint in Sunflower's eyes, that look that says he's deadly serious, and something bad is about to happen to someone.

"All of this, this whole meeting, playing, winning, losing, all of it."

CJ dropped his act immediately, "That's the way we've always done it. That's the way it has to be done."

"That's just it, it's the way it's always been done." Sunflower was grinning again. His teeth are almost as evil as he is. "I'd say that the biggest part of that is that we agree that's how it's done. So, if we agree to change things up, I think it'll change."

"What exactly did you have in mind?" CJ has eyes only for Sunflower now. Black Cat and Broken Mirror have stopped screwing around. They are scared.

Sunflower put all his chips in. "I'm all in, and I mean *all* in. I'm wagering my existence on this hand. If I lose, I'll just let myself go. I figured it out during one of our layovers in Vegas. Most of what keeps us going, what keeps our matter together, is the will to keep going on. For me, I've had it. I'm at the end. I want it all, or I want to be nothing. So if you win, off I go."

CJ could already see what the answer was going to be, but he asked anyway, "And if you win?"

"I expect the same from you. I win, you go."

CJ got officious, "There's more than just your pride involved. There is balance to be considered. You can't have things your way all the time. You just can't. If you did, the whole thing would collapse, and you'd go down with it."

"I don't care."

"What do you three think about it?"

Nobody says anything. Cat kicks me under the table. Mirror had taken his shades off and was mopping his brow furiously. I stammered, "This is news to me. If he wins, and you leave, I don't think any of us are going to stand a chance. I think he'll pick us off one by one and run things into the ground." I don't know where these words came from, but as soon as I said them, I knew they were true. Sunflower doesn't like us—he tolerates us.

"That's not true Tea," said Sunflower, with a wounded expression that fooled nobody. "I'm putting my ass on the line for *all* of us. If I win, we get the whole thing to ourselves. We can do whatever we want, whenever we want, to whomever we want. Besides, think of all those times I won it for us. More than my share, am I right? You guys owe me. At the very least, you owe it to me to stay out of this until it's settled."

Mirror, Cat, and me, we're not brave. We pull our antics from the cover of invisibility, from the shadows. We're happy to reap the rewards, but we don't want to risk anything. So, when challenged directly like this, we all turned meek. If spirits blushed, we'd all of us be crimson right now. None of us said another word. We just threw in our cards, and sat back from the table.

To his credit, CJ got his composure back remarkably fast.

"Do you understand what you're asking?"

Sunflower smiled wider. "Yep."

"Then I guess we'd better deal the cards. Throw in all your chips and turn your cards over. You want to play for everything, we're going to play it straight up."

Sunflower snapped his two cards face up on the table. King of clubs, and King of Spades.

CJ lets out a low whistle and laid his cards out in front of the others. Queen of Hearts, and Three of Diamonds.

I looked over at Cat and Mirror. They were wearing what I'm sure was the same expression I had—utter disbelief. How could CJ have agreed to this?

Jim starts dealing the flop. Snap. Three of clubs.

What the hell were we going to do if Sunflower won? We'd always been able to keep him in check, because CJ would always be there, winning his share.

Snap. King of hearts. CJ was all but done. Somehow, he was still smiling—it was a tight, grim variety, but a smile nonetheless.

Snap. Two of spades.

"You know CJ," Sunflower drawled, "I'm looking at these cards, and I'm feeling pretty good about myself. So good, in fact, I'm willing to change the bet slightly. If I win, you don't have to disintegrate or anything, but you'll butt out, and leave these three assholes to me. You forfeit the right to ever play again."

"Of course," he continued, with a glint in his eye as evil as his breath, "That would also mean you'd have to watch what I'm going to do."

"Watch the cards and shut your mouth, Sunflower. The stakes stay as is." CJ was deadly serious now. That serenity that he normally carried around him like a halo was completely gone. I wondered again if he knew something we didn't.

Snap. Queen of Clubs. Sunflower stopped grinning. "If you're fixing this somehow," he said—his voice shaking a little— "I win by default, you know that."

"They're your cards, and I haven't shuffled since you dealt."

There was one card left to deal.

The air around us when we'd arrived was thick with the smells of cut grass, sun-bleached cedar, and heavy dust. Somehow, it had gotten even closer in the room. We breathed it in, having all forgotten ourselves for the moment.

A noise outside caught my attention. It sounded like something heavy thumping. There was a pattern to it, but I couldn't figure out what it could be. I saw that Black Cat heard it, too. Whatever it was, the sound stopped a moment later, and we let it go. Jim was starting to turn the last card.

Suddenly, he paused. "Wait," he said, keeping his eyes locked on Sunflower's yellowed orbs, "You're absolutely sure you want this?"

"What, are you chickening out? My offer still stands CJ. Fold, and you get to live."

CJ didn't respond. Instead, he turned the card. Snap. King of Diamonds.

Victorious, the evil bastard stretched his grin to a grotesque width, as if he was unzipping the front of his face. We all have it in us to change our shape, but mostly we don't. It reminds us that we aren't like you. That we aren't human.

CJ did something odd then. He smiled back. It was as warm and genuine a grin as he'd worn when he'd done his silly cowboy act at the door. Leaning back in his chair, he took off his cowboy hat. With a wink, he flung his hat at me. Then he dissolved, falling apart like sand in the wind. I must still have been breathing, because I smelled a puff of leather and cinnamon.

The hat dropped with a soft thump in front of me. It was all that was left of Jim. Something made me pick it up. I was still fidgeting with it, twirling it around, when the winner started his gloating.

"Well folks," Sunflower's mouth was still gaping at the hinges. "Guess that's that. Things are going to be a little different around here, but don't worry—you'll still get your days. You just have to win them from me."

He was working the cards back into the pile now, shuffling. "Let's see… right now I've got mine, and I've got CJ's, which is enough to really have some fun. But I'm on a roll. I feel good. Things are happening for me, like I can't lose. So I'll ask all of you—wanna play, or do you just want to shoot those chips over here and save some time?"

That touched a nerve with Broken Mirror. "I've got forty days here, Sunflower," he whined, "If we give you everything, we'll starve, and I don't see you giving us anything back to live on, so yes, I'm going to play you for it."

Cat straightened up in her seat. Hearing her partner show such backbone inspired her.

"I'm in too." For once, there wasn't a trace of giggling in her voice.

"We've got ourselves a game here. Chai—you gonna play, or you gonna take the passive route like you always do? You can slide 'em over anytime."

Maybe it was the scent of CJ still in the air, or that the noise I'd heard from the outside had returned—stronger now—but I shook my head at Sunflower. With a toss of my wrist, I threw the Stetson up in the air, and dropped it as neat as could be on my head. CJ's words seemed to come out of my mouth, "Deal the cards, Sunflower"

We played. Each of us played our hands conservatively, imaginatively, brilliantly. The game went on and on. But three hours later, the results were exactly as Sunflower had predicted. He sat with every single chip in front of him, and this time, when he gave us his sick, grotesque grin, he went one step further, and threw back just the top of his head, and gave a huge belly laugh. It was something to see.

Mercifully, he pulled himself together before he started talking again.

"*Finally.* You know, I'm glad you guys decided to play. It's so much sweeter having all the days in front of me, knowing that I don't have to turn around and give any of it back."

I could hear Cat sobbing softly. Mirror was making comforting noises, and Sunflower continued, speaking directly to me.

"I was thinking of leaving you guys each a couple of days to get by on, but in the last half hour or so, I've thought better of it. Maybe you'll be a little more challenge next time if you're hungrier." He squeezed the cards, sending them flying in a scatter at Cat, saying, "Right, tubby?" She cried harder.

"As for me," Sunflower continued. At this point, I was still scared, but the old wish that he would shut up for two minutes was starting to come back.

Sunflower got to his feet, and walked to the dust-caked window. "I've got some plans of my own," he said. "And I realized that if I gave you idiots even one day a piece, you might figure out some way to screw it up again."

He motioned to the door without looking back at us.

"I want all of you to leave now. I've got work to do and, frankly, I can't wait to get started. If you think I've been rough in the past, you've haven't seen *anything.*"

He turned around. His eyes started to glow then, a sickly dark orange that ebbed and pulsed as he spoke … and *spoke.*

"There are so many people in this city. So many opportunities for mischief. *Real* mischief, mind. Not this piddly crap you guys do, and certainly not the little tricks I've pulled in the past. No, you're going to see some really bad things happening to a lot of really innocent people. It's going to be wonderful."

There'd been something nagging at me since Sunflower made his first move with CJ, and I couldn't put my finger on it. His rhapsodizing about the destruction to come, like a Bond-villain come to afterlife, had placed the final piece for me, and as brilliant a player as he was, as self-assured and aggressive as he could be, he was absolutely blind to the biggest flaw in his plan. The noise outside, which had become so loud that I was surprised that Sunflower wasn't hearing it, drove it all home for me.

I gave it one attempt. "Miniature Sunflower, I'm happy for you… beating CJ I mean. I am. I just think the things you're talking about are a little much. We're not meant to be doing these things. We're meant to make things uncomfortable. We make people realize how good they've got it most of the time. We mess with them. We even hurt them a bit sometimes, but what you're talking about is… it's not us."

"You're absolutely right, Chai. It's definitely not the jellyroll twins over there, and, let's call it what it is, it's definitely not you, Mr. Passive. Mr. Catch-them-when-their-back-is-turned. But you know what? It *is* me. It's me *all over*. I'm not like you. I'm meant for bigger and better things, and now I'm going to grab them."

Suddenly, he kicked a chair out of his way. The squeal of metal legs on concrete made me jump. Sunflower stalked toward the door.

"Alright," he said. "I'm tired of this. You've got to five to haul your asses out of here—all right, Mirror you get to seven, seriously man, you're disgusting—or we're going to play one last hand, for the same stakes I played with CJ. Right? Good. Now get out, or 'poof'.

He swung the door open then, and I saw the horses.

The entire shed smelled like a fridge gone bad just then, as Mirror, Cat, and I came as close to crapping our pants as we ghosts could get.

Mirror grabbed Cat's hand and squeezed. I couldn't move. I can't tell how I'd imagined them, but as terrifying as my darkest thoughts had been—seeing them in front of us was ten times worse.

"What the hell are you looking at?" snapped Sunflower.

"*Us.*"

The voice practically frosted the windows. One by one, they filed in. The first was stocky and wore a tight brown leather bomber jacket. He was chomping on a short, expensive smelling cigar, and had scars all over his stubbly face. He stood shorter than any of us, but gave off an aura of absolute feral rage, barely contained.

The next behind him was a striking, almost beautiful woman, with flowing silver blonde hair. She wore pale blue lipstick, and a long green kimono that clung to her curves. She kept dabbing at an enormous red sore at the side of her aquiline nose with an embroidered silk handkerchief. Somehow, her appearance was enhanced, rather than diminished by this flaw.

Three paces behind her was the thinnest man I'd ever seen. His suit was the height of fashion, but I couldn't see it fitting anyone else on the planet. He walked through the door. Two more people could have come through at the exact same time with room to spare. He wore a navy pinstripe suit, with immaculate white gloves, and had a slim black moustache over a completely unamused expression.

Their final member came in, and I took a step back so I could grab Mirror's other hand. Ducking through the doorway, *he* was seven feet tall at least, and seemed to block out the world behind him as he entered. He was a paper-white Viking in a tailored suit, and he only had eyes for Sunflower.

"You've been a very busy little ghost." His voice was deep and friendly, but there was a coldness in his tone that made me want to melt out through the cracks in the panelling.

His cohorts remained silent, but each seemed to be struggling against laughter. I could see the woman's handkerchief jiggling slightly as she hitched silently into it. The big man continued, "It looks like congratulations are in order."

To his credit, Sunflower wasn't going to take anything from anyone, even now. Whether this was bravery or monumental idiocy, I'll never know.

"Yeah, I won," he said, looking up at each of the horsemen in turn. "I took him down fair and square. I've got the days, and I'm going to use them."

The short guy mumbled around his cigar, "We heard."

The lady stopped chuckling, "Big plans."

The thin man was still smiling, "There's just one thing you seem to have overlooked."

I looked over at our tormentor of just a few minutes ago. His lunatic grin faltered a little, closing in around the corn kernel teeth as he started to understand. Cat whimpered a little just then, and looking around at her, at the weaklings he'd just dominated so completely, Sunflower shook his head, and drew himself up straight, stretching his torso so he was eye to eye with the blonde behemoth.

"Oh yeah? What would that be?"

There was a spark as the short guy relit his cigar on a flame from his thumb. "You've killed a lot of people, Mr. Sunflower."

"Too many, really, for what you are." The lady spoke around a large silver compact. Her sore had burst and she was busying herself with the cleanup.

"You see, Miniature, if I may be so bold," the thin man chimed in, "There's already someone that takes care of the particular function that you... ah... have expressed... *interest* in." He tittered, and the sound was enough to make my whole being want to fly apart.

Sunflower's voice cracked and rose sharply in pitch. He was nearly hysterical, but he remained defiant to the last, "And? So what?"

It looked as if he'd wanted to say more, but just then the giant wrapped his hand around Sunflower's entire torso and squeezed the whole body into his fist.

"*So, we're not hiring!*" And before Sunflower could even scream, the blonde man had bitten his head clean off to the neck. I mentioned before that we don't have bodies, so there was no blood, but we are made of matter, and when we play, we get dense enough to interact with things, and during these times, we can feel. Right now, those of us remaining felt sick. Cat groaned and became transparent. Mirror dropped my hand and lowered her to the floor as she went limp.

The rest of Sunflower's body dissipated, leaving behind a scent of rotten leaves and axle grease. The big man dusted off his hands, spat, and shook his head slightly, as if clearing out cobwebs. Then, without another look at us, he turned and the hulking incarnation of Death was gone.

Famine and Pestilence spared us a last disparaging glance and followed their partner out the door.

War looked us all up and down. His battle-scarred face was impossible to read. He didn't say anything for the longest time, and then finally he walked over to me.

"Well, cowboy," (I'd forgotten I was wearing the stupid hat,) "guess there's more to go around now. Quit looking so worried. You guys'll do fine."

Cat groaned as she started to come to.

He was walking out the door now, but turned one last time, "Just don't screw it up Jimmy. 'Cause we'll know." And then he was gone too.

Jimmy? He'd called me Jimmy.

The aroma of cut grass and cedar came back full on. They were warm, comforting smells, and I started to feel better about things. I felt a lot better, actually, and could sense something new. There were possibilities out there I'd never seen. I knew I wasn't going to have to cherry pick memories anymore. I was beyond those limits now. I understood so much about CJ now. It wasn't about winning at all, it never was.

I looked over at Cat and Mirror, who were still wavering in and out of opacity they were so scared.

"Relax guys. They're gone. Sunflower's gone. It's just us."

Mirror was first to recover, and I could see greed jumping up and down inside him, "Just us? We're going to have a ball." Cat was warming up to this, and I saw the same covetous look in her eyes.

I tipped my new cowboy hat and smiled at them. "Maybe yes, maybe no. Let's play some cards."

ADAPTATION

Life sign readings remained negative as the two men made their way through the strange, ruined Martian settlement. Doorways yawned into dark, angular structures.

"It's all so empty, sir. It gives me the creeps," said the young scientist.

"Survival of the fittest, Edgar," said Oderson. "That's what you're seeing here."

His assistant shook his head. "I don't know, Doctor. That seems like a callous way to look at it, the Martians, I mean…"

Oderson cut him off, "Survival, Edgar. Humans are the dominant species, and we've *earned* the right to prosper."

"But we destroyed our own planet, sir."

Oderson cocked an eyebrow. His assistant was bordering on impudence, but he decided to defeat the argument rather than simply pull rank.

"Edgar," began Oderson, speaking as one would to a child, "Human intellect designed the O_2 factories that made colonization possible, ergo: we are the dominant species."

The young assistant was gaping at him. He'd obviously been reading the propaganda sheets from the Eco-twits on Hoight1.

Enough was enough. "Had the Martians evolved, they would have been able to cope with the change in atmosphere. As it stands, they're dead, and we are standing on the richest new colony planet in a hundred years."

Edgar's voice quavered, and behind his face screen, Oderson could see the beginnings of tears.

"Two billion life-forms obliterated, Doctor," he moaned. "To imply that it was their *fault* somehow…"

"…is exactly how Pop-Control sees things, Edgar. Stop! We're here."

Oderson stood at the top of a shallow valley. Lying exposed before them on the scrub were thousands of glimmering gems of all colours and shapes. Despite numerous probes and tests on the surface, there was still no explanation for the phenomenon. Oderson and Johnson were the first humans to see it, and they would hopefully solve the mystery. *Regardless,* thought Oderson, *there's nobody left to argue about us claiming the lot.*

He stooped and picked up a ruby the size of his fist. It felt lighter than expected, not like stone at all. *Who cares?* he thought. It was worth a fortune.

Without warning, the stone exploded into a mass of jointed legs.

It skittered once around his palm, then sank dagger-like fangs deep into his fingers. The pain was immediate, and he went to his knees, swearing.

The field came alive with precious stones scuttling and rasping toward them. Sapphires became giant, scarab-like beetles. Diamonds sprouted wings and wicked looking stingers, taking to the air to form a beautiful, deadly cloud. Here and there, clusters of jewels revealed themselves to be immense, unnameable insect horrors. The sound of clicking legs and mandibles was deafening.

Cockroaches, thought Oderson, *like cockroaches after the nuke.*

Edgar fell to the ground, glittering, screaming, and dying.

Large, skinny-legged opal mantids began to claw their way up Oderson's leg. He slapped at them, and his hand came away studded with tiny onyx ant-things that were already sinking their pincers into him. He cried out and tried, like Edgar, to get away. The swarm surged, as if sensing his desire to flee, and he was covered from the waist down in beautiful, multifaceted death. Trying one more time to get away, he lurched forward, and slipped on the scrabbling things at his feet. He went down and was instantly engulfed.

As the bugs started to eat him, Oderson's mind detached. His consciousness started to float above his body. There was no more pain, even as the creatures began to devour his insides.

Staring up at the Martian moon, pale yellow against the darkening sky, he thought again about the survival of the fittest. *This time,* he thought, *we lost.*

TEMPTING MORSELS

Ada read the name of the bakery, and the phrase underneath again, and smiled. It read, "Venial Sins. It's not so bad to be so good!"

Inside, behind a short red counter, stood a tall, powerful looking man in a crimson apron. At the window, an elderly couple sat at a bleached oak table, sharing a slice of pumpkin pie, and sipping foamy, steaming cappuccinos.

"Good afternoon, Miss," said the man. Ada assumed he was the owner.

"It's Missus, actually," she replied, smiling.

"That's a shame." He winked; Ada felt hot blood colour her cheeks.

The man pushed a paper menu across the counter.

"What can we tempt you with today, *Missus?*"

She giggled. Alan never made her feel like this anymore. His brother Michael had—briefly—but that was years ago.

On the menu were five desserts, including chocolate mousse cake, white truffle tart, and her absolute girlhood favourite—butterscotch pie. She tapped the page. "I've never seen this anywhere else. Is it good?"

"Just like Grammy used to make," said the owner, winking again. She blushed again, but then had a discomforting thought—how had the man known her private name for her grandmother?

Before she could ask, the proprietor went swiftly behind a black velvet curtain, and returned less than a minute later with a small sliver of pie and a gleaming silver fork. Ada seated herself on a black vinyl stool. A moment later, he brought a tall glass of milk and set it beside the pie. The experience was complete—exactly as she remembered it from her childhood. The pie was creamy and sugary, its crust flaking and falling apart with ease. Each mouthful tasted better than the one before it. When she finally finished, her heart sank. Nothing, it seemed, would be as good ever again.

Without knowing she was going to, she spoke. "I'd sell my soul for another piece."

The owner laughed. "You'd have to."

"Pardon?" Ada sat up.

"One piece per customer." He laughed. "An odd rule, perhaps, but it serves." Her surprise must have been obvious, because he added, "Unless you're serious?"

Ada nodded, unable to help herself. She wanted this; she deserved it. Deserved a treat.

"Excellent." The man smiled, producing a contract.

She blanched.

"Oh, don't worry, missus." said the owner, "It's not forever—not for a piece of pie. It's just three minutes."

She signed.

He opened the curtain, and Ada walked through.

The owner laughed again. He nodded at the old man, "For in hell, one minute shall be as a thousand years, eh?"

There was no reply as the couple faded back to nothingness.

Three minutes later, the curtain parted, and the thing that had once been Ada stumbled through. She saw the pie waiting for her and began to shriek.

***

"Lookit that old lady," said the construction worker, looking out the window. "Been wanderin' around for years now. All she ever says is 'pie.' Sad how some folks get, huh?"

"Sad, indeed," said the man in the apron, nodding in acknowledgement. "How was your cake?"

"Fantastic," said the workman. "I'd kill for another slice."

"You'd have to."

TURN AROUND

Madness is following me.

I'm not being dramatic. There is something following me that wants me to go insane. I don't know if it's a ghost, a demon, or if it even has a name, but it's there. I know it is.

It started about a month ago. You know that sensation you get on the subway, or even just walking down the street—that absolute certainty that someone's watching you? It starts as a prickling at the base of your neck, then the tips of your ears get hot. You start to breathe more rapidly, and your heart speeds up. That's what it feels like for me all the time. All I have to do is turn around, and it'll be over, and I'll be insane.

That's the rule. Don't ask me how I know, I can't tell you. It, whatever *it* is, needs that moment of surprise. It needs me to whirl around and see it. That's how I've managed to stay a step ahead—I don't turn around anymore. What I do instead is turn left and take one step. Then, I turn left and take one step. If I'm travelling, at least a little bit, it can't catch me by surprise. That's what it needs.

"What about mirrors?" you might ask; I thought of that. Of course I did. It's no good. It's the same as turning left—if I'm not actively turning to confront it, it won't be seen.

It drove my wife, Patricia, crazy. I'd have to do a circle of the bedroom just to change my shirt. She insisted I see a shrink. I saw three of them, it never lasted. They each asked me to shut the door behind me, and I told them to go fuck themselves. The last one caught on and closed it for me. After listening to my story, though, he prescribed Zoloft, and, as I was leaving, called my name. I took a couple of lefts and told him where to go too.

When Patty found out that I stopped going, she left me for good. It was about three weeks ago now, and whatever this thing, this phenomenon is—it's getting worse. I don't know how much longer I can last.

The thing plays tricks, too. Two weeks ago, I was in the mall, and suddenly I was smelling Kelly McNeil's perfume. It was that light vanilla scent that was so big in the nineties. The smell seemed to suddenly be all around me, and I was barraged by memories: nuzzling Kelly's neck, the taste of her skin, and the feel of her lips. For a few seconds, I could even feel her breath on my neck. Hell, I could even smell the sour apple candies she was always eating. I didn't turn around. That was hard.

It was even harder last week, when suddenly someone stuck a gun in my back.

"Turn around," said a gruff man's voice. "Or I'll shoot you where you stand."

I didn't turn around, and it eventually went away—though I'd say I'm well and truly screwed if I get mugged for real.

Now, the thing has stopped playing tricks. It's realized that pushing me makes it easier to resist. Instead, it's just there, prickling my neck, heating my ear tips, and it's never gone. I sleep on my back, and it feels like it's in the mattress, watching me.

Yesterday was my last day at work. They cited downsizing, but it's obvious. Looking back just briefly at the way I've behaved—turning my desk around so everyone has to approach me in profile, and breathing hard almost all the time, because I can feel the presence there, just… fucking… *staring* at me.

I'd have fired me in an instant.

I'm making this recording because it's over. The thing wants me insane, and I'm really close. In trying to save my mind, I've become obsessed. It won't let me stop thinking about it. Everywhere I go, no matter where I am, no matter what I'm doing, it's there. When I sit down in the bathroom, it's perched on the goddamned toilet tank behind me.

So… I'm going to turn around, and face whatever this beast, demon, ghost, whatever it is. I'm sorry Patty. Maybe, once someone finds me, and checks me into an asylum someplace, I'll get well one day, and try to give you a call. I love you.

I'm turning around now.

Huh…

How about that? It's a puppy.

Just a cute little brown and black puppy, sitting there with his tongue hanging out. Looks like he's smiling too.

Imagine that.

I've been so scared, and it's just been this... this puppy... this cute little puppy following me all along.

Just a puppy. Hee hee.

Just a puppy. I can't believe it!

Just a puppy. I can't...

Just a puppy... Just a puppy... Just a puppy... Just a puppy... Just a puppy... Just a puppy... Just a puppy...

FEAR COMBINED

"What's it doing now, doctor?"

"Sleeping, I think, sir."

The soldier peered through the Lexan window. His eyes were drawn in the dark to a faint flicker of movement. "All of it?" he asked.

"No. Look over there, sir." The scientist was pointing at the wall, where the thing's tail slithered and probed at the seams of its cell.

"Jesus." Captain Jameson set his face against the chill that threatened to overwhelm him. Seeing the thing up close was unnerving. Seeing it move was something else entirely. He considered himself a thoroughly modern, secular man, but this act of creation tugged at deep-seated beliefs he'd thought gone forever.

"I know, sir. It's fascinating, isn't it?" The scientist was smiling broadly now, "The next round of tests will really show us what it can do." He was gesticulating wildly at the Captain, growing louder and breathier as he continued, "The first round was exciting too, of course, but those were just so we could find out how to subdue the thing. I'm really excited to see what it's capable of."

Jameson grabbed the scientist roughly by the arm, "Dr. Evans, this isn't a game."

The thin man went nearly as pale as his lab coat. "Of… of course, sir. I wasn't implying…" He swallowed, took a deep breath and continued, "All precaution will be taken, sir."

"See that it is, doctor." He relaxed his grip, "And can't we get some more light in here? This is a military facility, isn't it?"

Evans, still shaken, shrugged his shoulders, "The generators are acting up, sir. The weather out here is playing hell with them." He looked back at the cage, "But we left the lights on in here, as we thought if it could be encouraged to remain asleep…"

"Fine," Jameson cut him off. "Go prep the tests, and I'll see you back here at oh-six-hundred sharp." The Captain turned back to the Lexan cage. Evans was non-military, but didn't argue with the order and hurried along the corridor.

"Fascinating." Jameson repeated. That was one word for it. He tried again to make out distinct forms in the dim light. He moved closer, pressing his forehead to the warm surface. The musky scent of animal hung thick in the air. Growing accustomed to the light now, he followed the queer, broad contours of its ursine lower body.

"See anything you like, Captain?"

Jameson started. The voice had come from within the cage. He'd been so concerned with the details, he'd completely missed the thing coming full awake. It was studying him now, reflecting back the light in four perfect cat's eyes. Jameson, in that moment, felt disquietingly similar to a mouse.

"Rivers?" He couldn't believe that the thing remembered.

"Yes, she is part of us," said the beast. It came forward into the light, revealing its terrible, beautiful asymmetry. "But you'd know about that, wouldn't you, Captain Jameson?"

His alarm must have shown, because it laughed. It was a tinkling, feminine sound that gave him chills. "You're the one who volunteered us for this, weren't you?"

Jameson struggled for a response. He decided on a form of the truth, "You were dead, Rivers. No next of kin, an ideal candidate."

"And you thought this was something I'd want, did you?" she asked, purring. From beside her, though, came a low, rumbling growl that was pure menace. "What I really want to know, Captain, is now that you've got us here, what do you want with us?" She ran a finger down the corner of the cell, "We're bored."

Jameson had suddenly had enough. The feeling of being toyed with was unbearable. He thumbed the walkie at his shoulder, and as calmly as possible said, "Evans, it's awake. Gas it now." The thing's reaction made him feel better at once. Pouty, feminine lips drew back around a mouthful of sharp teeth in a snarl. From her lion's head came a bellowing roar he felt in his bowels. Deep white scratches appeared in the Lexan wall as she raked her claws down the inside of the chamber. Silent white fog rolled in from above, obscuring her features. There was a massive thud near the lock, and he looked down to see the anaconda tail withdrawing. The attacks on the wall began to weaken.

"See you tomorrow," said Jameson, watching intently. Seconds later, the beast slumped to the floor, and he went to check on Evans' preparations.

***

That night, Jameson lay awake considering his conversation with the monster. Seeing it (no… HER, his mind insisted) face to face had brought back ideas and arguments he'd thought long since settled. Hearing her voice though, so articulate, yet so changed… it worried him.

When sleep finally took him, his dreams took him back to the moment of creation. He watched again as Sergeant Rivers was bathed in the untested rays of the Moreau device. He still didn't understand the mechanics of it, but knew it had something to do with dormant parts of the DNA strand getting woken up.

Pulsing indigo light filled the room. Miraculously, the flesh began to knit itself together, erasing all trace of the IED shrapnel. Sinews knotted together. Pink scar tissue formed, darkened, and became smooth and perfect once more.

Seconds later, her eyes flew open, making everyone jump. A moment later, she began to scream. The changes were abhorrent to watch, but Jameson hadn't turned away for a second. It was by his signature that this woman was here now. That made it his responsibility to watch, and witness everything.

No, he hadn't slept well at all.

***

Currently, Evans was doing the introductions. The entire team had assembled this morning for the tests. The assembled soldiers and thinkers had been chattering wildly amongst themselves. Even the sopping weather outside hadn't dampened their spirits. They stood like a tour group at the zoo, looking out the window again and again to catch a glimpse of what was to come. It was giving him a headache. Jameson sipped his third coffee and walked over to the window with the rest of the gawkers. The cage had been shrouded in black cloth. These damned scientists and their theatrics, he thought.

"… and, of course, we couldn't have done any of it without the Moreau device." Evans was practically chirping. He gestured at the impressive chrome and plastic machine that had been brought up from the lab specifically for this little speech. "For the first time in man's history, we have harnessed and controlled what can only be described as 'magic.' Let me elaborate for a moment, if you will. What are X-rays, microwaves, radio waves, but invisible energies…"

Jameson sat up. He wasn't watching the doctor, and was tuning him out as best he could. The cage was moving. From somewhere distant, he could still hear the storm raging outside.

"… were able to observe a single, measurable phenomenon…" Evans continued. Trust the scientist to make magic sound boring.

The cage shifted back and forth. It's trying to tip it over, thought Jameson. Amazing. Before last night, he would have assumed this was simply a consequence of the thing's massive size, but now he wasn't so sure.

Jameson glanced now at the door facing the cage. In just fifteen minutes, that door would open, and then these people would really see what the situation was. He downed the rest of his cup. Academics, he snorted softly to himself, they won't understand until they see blood.

"… recreated with this astounding device right here. By focusing…"

The Captain heard the thing's silken voice in his mind again, "See anything you like?" He rubbed the space between his eyes. This whole project had the potential to go very, very wrong. When Jameson looked into the arena again, the cage was rocking. One side was raising several inches off the ground with each jolt from within.

"… proud to introduce Captain Ronald Jameson. Captain Jameson?"

Time to focus. Jameson tore his gaze from the cage and walked to the podium. The lights glared in his eyes, and he felt their heat prickling on his forehead. He opened his mouth to begin, but just then the lion's roar shattered the silence. Everyone jumped. Thank you, Private, he thought. He couldn't have asked for a better way to get their attention.

He began, "Well, that's as good a place to begin as any." There were some nervous chuckles at that. He cut them off with a look.

"We are at war with an enemy that does not fear us. Our enemy does not fear death. An enemy without fear is impossible to defeat. Therefore, to win against terror, we must become terrifying."

There was a crash from the arena. The cage had overbalanced at last. Patience, thought Jameson, you'll be in the spotlight soon enough. He cleared his throat.

"What you are about to see is a prototype, an enemy for our enemy. If the tests go well here today, we will soon have a small squadron of these special troops to be deployed immediately into the remote regions where we believe the enemy to be concentrated. After that, may their god have mercy on their souls."

He moved to the open viewing window and thumbed a remote that sat on the ledge. The plain metal door swung open, and a heavily built man in a prison jumpsuit staggered into view. "This is Kelvin Gross. Convicted murderer," Jameson spoke without turning, "He killed nine people with his bare hands, including three while he was locked up. He received the death penalty last week. Obviously the needles were loaded with placebo, but in the eyes of society he no longer exists."

He pushed the second button on the remote. Out in the arena, beyond hearing, the lock on the cage released. The curtain was supposed to have risen at this point too. But, as predicted, it was trapped under the cell.

It didn't matter; the beast was out. Jameson marvelled at the grace of the beast despite the incongruous parts that made up its body.

The man in the arena below didn't stand a chance. Covering the space in brief moments, the Chimerax pounced. The closed-circuit feed in the viewing room relayed the action in gruesome close-up detail. Jameson pressed a button on his remote and the scene froze. The plasma screen was filled with Kelvin Gross' face, pulled into a grotesque mask of pure terror.

"That, Gentlemen, is why we've done all this," he said. The assembled group turned from the brutal spectacle beyond the glass. Most of their faces had drained of colour. One of the younger scientists appeared to be fighting the urge to vomit.

Jameson continued, "This man, this killer, is afraid for his life. Look at that expression. Fear will win this war."

He turned back to the viewing window, "The second reason is obvious."

There was a massive thud as something hit the glass. He couldn't have planned it better. Gross' torso dropped away from the window with a wet plop. The Chimerax had been busy while he'd waxed philosophical. Both of its heads were streaked with gore, and pieces of prisoner were everywhere.

"Most effective, wouldn't you agree?" Jameson looked over his shoulder, "It is the ultimate blending of science and the supernatural. We're playing for keeps gentlemen. Dr. Evans, cut the switch and bring it back up here. We'll leave you to your performance tests." He handed the remote to the scientist, who promptly dropped it.

"Er, thank you, Captain Jameson." Evans stooped to retrieve the device. "I forgot to mention that part. We needed a way to ensure that no innocents would be harmed." Bolstered by the opportunity to recite fact, his voice steadied, "We implanted a neuro-electric stunner. A tiny chip that, when activated, will render the beast unconscious."

He pressed a button on the remote. The reaction from below was immediate. Sergeant Rivers' human head snapped back, then went limp. The rest of the beast was unfazed. If anything, the insult to part of its body made the rest of it angrier. Turning to face the viewing window, the lion roared again, and the anaconda twined around its waist.

Jameson faced the scientist, "Dr. Evans, did you install a chip in each of the heads, or just the human one?"

In response, Evans eyes flicked toward the door.

"ANSWER THE QUESTION DOCTOR!" Jameson couldn't believe the stupidity of the man, or the cowardice.

"We… we assumed the human brain would naturally assert control, sir. We believed if we disabled the human, we'd disable the beast."

"What a waste," said Jameson. "Soldiers, ready arms."

The security detail lined up along the window, rifles at the ready.

Jameson gave Evans a look that said, I hope you're happy.

There was a tremendous crash from outside. The building shook with the force of the thunderclap. The lights went dead. The generators—shit, thought Jameson. He looked at the mag-locked door separating this room from the arena. The indicator lights were out. In the arena, emergency lights cast their high-beam spotlights on the ground, partially illuminating the carnage, leaving the rest in shadow.

They had to act fast. "Shoot to kill men. Move out." He ordered them through the door.

The six men filed through the door on either side of the glass and spread out, preparing to flank the beast. A moment later, they were in position and their automatics let loose with a hail of bullets. The Chimerax charged.

Jameson shot a look at Evans. He had his own sidearm out and levelled it at the good Doctor now.

"Doctor, we've got just a few seconds before that thing gets in here. If it does, I'm going to shoot you first. How do we stop it?"

The gangly scientist swallowed once and passed out.

Typical, thought Jameson. With a huge leap, the Chimerax reached the viewing window with its clawed hands. The soldiers closed in, firing repeatedly. Like a grotesque pennant, the head of the anaconda came into view. With lightning speed, it swept from side to side, and wrapped two men up in its coils. They barely had time to scream as the breath was crushed from their lungs and they were flung against the window. After just two more hits, the window smashed, and the beast pulled its terrible bulk into the room. The lights in the room flickered on and off. The backup generator had apparently survived, but it was struggling against the load.

Jameson backed up. The lab coats were stampeding the exit like cattle. The Chimerax lunged forward and the tiny fat man at the back of the pack fell. In the excitement, the electric stun had worn off, and "Kim" had woken up again. Now her feral screams of rage mingled with the lion's roar as she sunk her pointed teeth into the meat of her prey.

Got to be something, thought Jameson. He looked around frantically, not daring to fire his own weapon for fear of drawing the thing's attention.

The room, so clinical and orderly minutes ago, was a slaughterhouse. The thing was as efficient as it was strong. With a single swipe of its arms, men fell to the floor where the heads finished the job.

Jameson took another step away from it, backing into something that rattled and rolled away on tiny wheels. It was the Moreau device.

The exit door lock kept engaging and releasing with each surge of power. It made a hollow metallic clang each time. Finally, the man at the front kept pulling until the next surge released the lock again. It opened slightly, then was slammed back home in the crush from behind, where colleagues were being slashed and eaten alive.

There was a click-hum from behind Jameson, and the Moreau device illuminated the room with a flash of blue light. It got the Chimerax's attention. Even from across the room, he could make out the grin on her gore-streaked face.

"What are you doing, Captain?" she asked. The anaconda dropped its most recent victim and coiled around her waist. "Something interesting, I hope. These ones die too easily."

Jameson didn't answer. Since the machine had gone off, his gun had started vibrating with energy.

The Chimerax started moving closer. Jameson knew it could close the gap in an instant, but it wasn't. It's toying with me, he thought. I amuse it. He raised the gun, aiming for the lion's head first.

The monster laughed. "More stings?" Suddenly, the anaconda reared. The woman shifted her gaze to the machine, "What have you done?" the snake hissed at him. It was a horrifying voice, like stones grating together.

That's new. Jameson shuddered and pulled the trigger. The lion's face disintegrated in a spray of blood and fur.

The woman's scream was beyond human. Several of the surviving crowd, who had taken this time to organize and get the door open again, held their ears with their hands.

The Chimerax launched itself at him. He got off two more shots. The first went wild, but the second caught the thing in its shoulder. It staggered back with the pain. Jameson took aim at the human head, at Rivers.

Suddenly, a truck hit him in the chest. He huffed out almost all his air in with the sudden impact. Looking down, he saw the anaconda wrapped around his ribs. He felt like an empty beer can, about to implode. By sheer luck, his gun was still free. He socked it hard against the scaled body and fired. A huge hole appeared in the snake. Kim screamed again as the top half of the snake dropped to the ground. He found its flailing head and put another bullet in it. Two down, he thought, but before he could finish, Rivers was at him. She raked his arm with her heavy claws, and the gun fell to the ground. He staggered back.

"I'm going to enjoy this Joseph," said the Chimerax. "I'm going to eat your entrails while you watch for what you've done to us."

Jameson felt his consciousness waver. He groped behind him for something to steady himself. He upset the metal trolley that held the Moreau device. It crashed to the ground. Just then, the lights flicked, then came on full and the machine hummed to life. Energy flooded his body. It felt warm and good, like a summer's day erupting from his stomach. His shredded arm knit itself back together, and he felt strong.

The Chimerax flew at him in a rage, claws bared. Jameson rolled to the side and the beast crashed into the Moreau transmitter. Something inside made the hollow pop of a light bulb going dead.

Without thinking, Jameson advanced and punched the creature as hard as he could. Ribs cracked and the beast wheeled around. Rivers screamed in fury. Jameson shot forward and grabbed her by the throat. He squeezed. She stared wildly, and managed, "Captain, please don't!" Jameson focused on the ruins of the lion's head to avoid the wild, panicked stare of the woman he'd once known. Claws raked his back as it tried to get free, but he held on. The attacks grew weaker and weaker until, finally, the monster fell limp to its knees before collapsing on its remaining face.

Unwilling to take chances, Jameson retrieved his gun and shot the thing until he was satisfied. He then contemplated the scene. There were over a dozen men and women lying dead by the door, and of course, the monstrosity at his feet.

Now that the danger was past, Jameson felt some of the adrenaline leaving his body. He was crashing *hard*. The muscles in his forearm ached. These were just the start though, as, within seconds, everything was contracting. He tried to remain conscious, to figure out what was going on, but to no avail. Jameson swayed, then sat down hard on the ground. Grey fog swirled at his periphery while fire burned in his veins. Finally, his senses overloaded, and he passed out.

***

"What's it doing, Doctor?"
"Sleeping, I think."
"All of it?"
"Yeah. We were damned lucky, sir. For awhile there it looked like we were through."

Jameson stirred at the voices. Evans was here. Evans would know what the hell was going on. He tried to get to his feet and promptly fell back down. His balance was completely off. A new sound made him prick up his ears. There was a heavy, moist panting coming from somewhere nearby. He held his breath, trying to listen. To his shock, his chest kept moving. Something tickled his cheek. He turned and saw himself.

The lion's roar drowned out his screams of "Evans!!" Jameson clawed at the Lexan wall of the cage, to no avail. Suddenly, he became aware of his other senses, and his other thoughts. Even as the gas hissed in from above, he was formulating his plan for escape.

MOPPING UP

All things considered, Tim would rather have been at the dump.

There he'd be driving a truck, or a bulldozer, or something else menial and mindless. In other words, the hard work was already over.

Instead, he was here, in another small town, with stale gas mask air filling his lungs, working another Door-to-Door Detail. They had to "sanitize" the residential areas so that the surviving population would have somewhere to live that wasn't a crowded barracks.

Standing in front of 26 Watkins Way, Tim verified the address against his list. It was a formality, as the presence inside had been noted with a "Z" spray painted over the expensive looking hardwood double doors.

He shoved the often-folded list back into his pocket, chambered a round in his Beretta, and tried the knob. It was locked. The windows had been boarded up from the inside, but the double doors seemed to be relying on two large deadbolts to keep it shut. *I should wait for the battering ram,* he thought, drawing his gun. He *should* wait—but he just wanted this last job done so he could go home. "Voluntaries" were allowed private quarters; it was the one benefit to this job.

Tim fired five shots into the locks, then kicked the door open and went inside.

The reek of death and decay was an almost tangible presence, permeating every bit of skin the mask didn't cover. He fought the urge to gag.

To the left of the door, his eyes were drawn to an artist's easel in the middle of the room. The paper was torn along the right edge, and there was an awful smear of brownish-red obscuring the page, but he could still make out the cartoonish purple teddy bear flying a kite. Underneath, painted text was readable between the bloodstains:

```
Wally Bea he pretty kite all day long.
```

Copies of a children's book with the same bear on the cover were piled on the floor. The author was listed as "Dylan Mackie".

A noise from the staircase in the hall made him turn. Coming down the stairs in slow, jerky movements was a cat. It had an angry, bald red gouge on its back, and was missing an eye. Looking at Tim, the cat bared teeth that still looked sharp. It started descending faster. The Beretta jumped once in Tim's hand and the cat dropped in a heap. Suddenly, he became aware of a tapping sensation around his feet. Looking down, Tim saw eight soot coloured mice trying to chew through his boot—they all had the telltale twitchy movements of infection. *This is insane,* thought Tim, *insane*. He lifted his boot and brought it down, crushing three of them. Another had made it almost to the top of his right boot, and he shook it to the floor and finished it as well.

Moving into the kitchen, Tim's eyes fell on the cat's food bowl in the middle of the floor. It was full to overflowing from a bag of kibble that stood open beside it. Beyond that, in a corner breakfast nook, was a typewriter with a single sheet of paper loaded, and a heavy looking revolver. His curiosity piqued, Tim went to the table and read:

```
Wally and the Kite
Hands shaking so much. It hurts. So hard to
think.
Johanna's dead. She bit me. Had to shoot her.
Dear Lord help me. Know what I must do, but
csn't can't pull the trgger.
Will lock myself in. Coward.
```

And then something that made Tim's blood run cold:

```
Was a unded man
Had a undead cat
It caught a undead mous
An they all lived together
In a litle undead house
Some 1save me
Some 1 kill me
```

While Tim had been reading, the man himself had appeared. Standing at the door of the kitchen, Dylan Mackie looked like a man with a terrible hangover. His first action was to lope jerkily to the bag of cat food. He bent over and fell to his knees. The zombie took a handful of kibble out of the bag and dropped it on the pile. Tim was transfixed. *Just a normal guy, taking care of his cat.* thought Tim, then, *this sucks.*

Mackie, who had written about Wally the purple teddy once upon a time, staggered to his feet and finally noticed his house guest. Tim fired twice—one shot caught the man in the shoulder, and the other tore off his left cheek, spattering the green cardigan he wore with thick black clots of blood. Mackie lurched forward. Without the ravages of the outside world, his muscles hadn't degraded much, and he was faster than Tim had become used to.

Tim pulled the trigger and heard only a hollow click, and then Mackie was on him. His jacket and gloves wouldn't tear, but the writer was reaching for his mask. This close, Tim could see deep purple black circular bruises on the man's temple and under his chin.

(can't pull the trigger. Coward.)

Tim staggered back into the table. He got a foot up and shoved Mackie back across the kitchen. He grabbed the revolver from the table and, as Mackie tottered toward him, he prayed and fired at the same time. Black blood and brain spattered the white kitchen cupboards, and Dylan Mackie was down.

Glancing again at the note, Tim made up his mind, pulling the cover off the table and draping it over the body. He went briefly back to the living room, and brought the small rotted body of the cat, and put that under the blanket with its onetime owner. For lack of anything more profound to say, Tim crossed himself and said, "Sorry, man. You seemed like a really nice guy."

On his way out, he stopped one last time to pick up the copies of "Wally Bear's Picnic" from the table. He was going to make sure every kid he knew got to read that book.

A FAIRY TALE

On the borders of a deep, dark wood lived the gentlest woman that ever was. She lived with her stepmother, who was wicked to her.

The young woman, Annabelle, was kind to the animals and birds of the forest, but her suffering made them sad.

One day, a phoenix flew in her window. It turned a single, lazy gyration, and alighted on her sill.

"I've come to make you happy, Annabelle," it said.

"How is that?" asked Annabelle.

"By setting fire to your stepmother's bed."

"Oh, that *would* be delightful."

"Will you sing while I burn?"

"Of course."

TREASURES OF THE DEEP

"She's coming," said Keith, training the binoculars on a spray of foam in the distance.

"She'd better be," came a voice from just above the water. "I'm not putting this outfit on again."

"Shut up, Mike," said Keith. "We're only going to get one shot at this." He glanced at his partner in the water, who was draped with over twenty pounds of seaweed. They'd had to fill airbags and shove them into Mike's wetsuit to keep him afloat. The ruse was perfect, though. There was no sign that anyone else was nearby. Keith looked to be perfectly adrift, though the heavy weight attached to the underside was keeping his movement to a minimum.

He sharpened the focus on his binoculars, and studied the mermaid coming toward them through the surf. Everything was happening the way the old man at the bar said it would.

***

"Can't resist a fellow in distress," the old sailor had said, cackling and swigging deep from the third drink Keith had purchased for him. "It's true!"

Keith had the sense he was hearing secrets men would have died for not too long ago. Funny, though, how age, addiction, and loneliness would drive a man's price down.

Mike and Keith had heard the stories of mermaids rescuing lost sailors before. They'd devoted months to collecting any and all stories about the creatures. What they were after with old Captain Rummelton was a piece of lore they'd never heard before.

"Tell us, Captain," Mike had said, "about the eyes."

The old man got very quiet then, realizing he'd said too much. One drink later, he gave up, and said, "If a man loves a mermaid, and a mermaid loves a man, her magic will protect him under the sea, and he can swim as if he'd been born a fish."

"And the eyes, Captain?" Mike insisted.

The old man sighed, and Keith had his first pang of guilt.

"The power's in their eyes, lad," said the old sailor. "Take and hold the eyes, and the result's the same." He was staring at the table now, and wouldn't look up.

"Do me a favour—leave me be now. Please."

***

Keith stowed the binoculars. It... she... was almost here, and he had to look as helpless as possible. He lay back on the raft.

Waiting was intolerable. If Keith had had more patience, he and Mike wouldn't be on this insane path to quick wealth. What might have been thirty seconds, or thirty minutes later, he heard a disturbance in the water close to his thighs.

"You poor thing." said the mermaid. Her voice was soft and melodious, like the soft lapping of waves on a beach at sundown. The effect this had on Keith was immediate and alarming. His water-soaked pants felt too tight, and he sat up to confront his would-be rescuer. He took one look at the mermaid, and found he was unable to speak. They had expected she'd be beautiful—that had been a constant in the stories—but this was simply unfair.

The mermaid was feminine perfection. She had the body of a sex goddess, with soft womanly curves, high, firm breasts that were just the right size for someone who lived in the water. She'd pulled herself up on the raft, and sat there, looking at him, completely unselfconsciously. Keith could see the legends had gotten a very important fact wrong. The tail started much lower down; she was woman enough to make his every dream come true.

The mermaid's face was the distillation of every innocent girl-next-door that Keith had ever pined for. She wore concern in the shape of her lips and the arch of her eyebrows. Her eyes, though, were all Keith could see. Where the whites should have been, her eyes were seawater green. The colour shifted and changed in the light, and made her black irises seem to float like tiny islands in a magical tempest. She pulled a long, lustrous lock of auburn hair behind her ear and smiled at him.

Keith reached out to her, and she clasped his hand in her own. Her skin was warm. She opened her mouth to speak. Instead, she screamed. It was a broken, anguished cry, and blood began to run freely from the corner of her mouth. A moment later, the stainless-steel point of Mike's harpoon emerged between the mermaid's breasts. It grew and grew, like a whale breaching the waves, dragging freshets of blood behind it. The mermaid tried to draw a breath, found she could not, and collapsed between the two men.

"We got her!" shouted Mike. "I don't believe it, we got her!" He smacked the floor of the raft in triumph. "Great job man!"

Keith couldn't reply; he'd buried his face in his hands.

***

"So… did it work?" asked the young sailor.

"Yeah, it worked," said Keith, scratching again at his white-stubbled cheek. He was so tired these days. "The old captain left something out. Taking out the mermaid's eyes put a curse on us."

He pushed the glass container across the table. "We went to the bottom of the ocean," said Keith. "We found a fortune too, but everyone on our boat was dead when we got back to the surface—killed in a freak storm."

Keith spun the jar to look at the contents, and the contents looked back. "We tried a half-dozen times, and it happened each and every time."

"So why keep it?" asked the younger man.

"A reminder," replied Keith. He wanted a drink. He wanted to go to bed. "That's why I keep my eye in a pickle jar—to remind me that I saw a miracle once…" he trailed off then. The young man waited awhile, before leaving him in awkward silence.

Keith kept looking at his prize. "I saw a miracle," he said again, to no one in particular, "and I killed it."

FREEDOM WITHIN REACH

Edgar collapsed back against the wall. He was so close—inches, really, but those inches made all the difference.

His shoulders ached. Straining against his bonds had used up the meagre energy that he'd been able to muster. It had been fourteen months since the Duke had jailed him, and Edgar had spent every minute since then in agony.

He stared at the heavy, wooden cell door. It was barely visible in the waning light from the minuscule barred window above them. Edgar cursed the Duke again, fourteen months and counting for an imagined slight.

The Duke's daughter had smiled at Edgar when crossing the street. Only smiled. Edgar, who had been grooming a horse at his stable, had smiled back. The Duke had witnessed this exchange and, in a moment of pique, had accused Edgar of stealing from his customers.

Sweat pooled on Edgar's lip. He licked the moisture greedily. The guards wouldn't be offering him any water for another two hours. He made another attempt to close the gap, and still he came up short.

His cellmate groaned. Maximilian couldn't talk. Charged with blasphemy, the Inquisitors had crushed his tongue flat in an iron vice. Maximilian, driven insane, now communicated only by moaning. At first Edgar had been sympathetic, but after a few days the constant slavering monotone of his only companion was eating away at his sanity.

Edgar slept. He had fitful dreams—those had changed, too—his dreams. When he'd first arrived, he had dreamed of riding his horse across the valley, of fishing in the brook, of life's simple pleasures.

Now, his dreams were always the same: the guards had left his leg chain unlocked. It was a simple dream, but all the worse for that very reason. He'd woken countless times, expecting to see the manacle gone. Feeling it very much intact always crushed his spirits anew.

The next morning, he awoke, and this time something was different. For whatever reason, he saw the cell illuminated in the morning light, and knew that today he would reach. Once he'd captured those last inches, he would be free.

Carefully, Edgar stretched out along the floor. The stones were sweating in the morning sun, and his dirty tunic was quickly soaked through. He crawled closer to his goal.

Finally, reaching the end of his chain, he found his goal still within reach—Maximilian, still asleep, lay closer than ever before. Keeping absolutely quiet, Edgar laid his callused palm across the mute, moaning bastard's throat, and began to squeeze. The man flailed, but his death throes sounded the same as any of his other plaintive sounds, and no one came to his aid. Edgar added his other hand, and felt the man's neck spasm hard beneath his grip and grow still.

Relieved tears streamed down Edgar's face. It was silent in the cell—*silent*. He was finally free of the incessant, grating moaning.

Now he could concentrate on the damnable guards.

THE CABIN SLEEPS

"Who lives there, Mommy?" Becky was standing on the grass, pointing to a small, decrepit board cabin. "I don't think anyone lives there, sweetie," she replied.

"Where are the windows?" her daughter asked, walking closer. Karen stiffened, suddenly positive that this crumpling brown shack was a very bad place.

"They're behind those boards. Come on now," she said. "I want to show you the creek where I used to play before it starts raining." That got Becky moving, but as they started down the beach, Karen looked back once more. The old clapboard building looked like a rotted stump poking through the beach, something full of maggots and termites. Karen shivered and rubbed her arms. Something struck the back of her neck and she let out a little scream. The something trickled down her back. Rain.

Another drop hit her on the shoulder, and then all of them were running back down the beach to their cottage. As Karen watched Becky's little feet kicking up sand below her bright yellow shorts, she was filled to bursting with emotion.

"Run, run, run!" She called, laughing, and all thoughts of the cabin disappeared. As they reached the safety of Uncle Robert's guest cottage, the skies opened up.

That night, after Becky was asleep, Karen sat in the screened-in porch, watching the storm and smoking a joint. Between the lightning strobing across the lake, the accompanying thunder and the rustling of trees shaking briskly in the whipping wind, she didn't hear the screen door opening, or Bob coming up behind her. He pinched the joint out of Karen's fingers just as she finished taking a hit.

"Good evening, young lady," he said. She looked up at her uncle, stricken dumb. A second passed, then two, and then she shattered the silence with a wicked coughing fit. The smoke swirled once, then dissipated in the breeze through the window screens.

"Relax, kid," said Robert, "I'm not your dad." He took a long draw on the joint and crushed out the roach in the ashtray. With the pained, pinched voice of a veteran smoker, he asked her, "How was your first day out?"

Still a little shaken from the surprise, and the sudden relief, she said, "Not bad. We just walked up the beach a little and saw that creepy looking cabin. I didn't remember it, though."

Robert sat down in the empty Muskoka chair next to her. "That place? It used to scare the hell out of you when you were a kid. It's the old McLaren place. Why?"

She replied, "Becky was interested in it, but I didn't let her go near. It just felt, I don't know, weird or something."

Robert's face darkened. He said, "Don't let her go near there, Karen. That place is so old and weather-beaten, it could fall apart at any moment."

"I got that much, it looks terrible," said Karen, "But I'm talking about something else. I just got a bad feeling when I looked at it."

Her uncle pulled out his cigarettes and lit one, sitting back in the chair. He gave his niece a small smile, "There's a story alright, but I feel like we ought to be around a campfire before I tell it."

Karen smiled back, "You can't say there's a story, and then not tell it Robert. Come on."

Robert was silent for a moment, and then he sighed. "All right," he said, "I'll tell you the short-short version, so you'll keep Becky the hell away from it, okay?"

They nodded, and he began, "A man named Alvin McLaren and his wife lived up here. They weren't summer people; they stayed in that little shack even in the winter. It was built a long time ago, and the waterline was a lot further out, in case you're wondering about the beach all around it. Anyway, they had a little girl named Elizabeth. Alvin, he loved that little girl, doted on her night and day, so it's said.

"One day, he was meant to be watching the girl, but he was around the back chopping wood. It was fall, and the water was rough. The little girl waded out into the water and couldn't get back in. At that time of year, she wouldn't have lasted too long, just enough to scream once or twice. Alvin didn't hear her. Shelley came home some time later, and he was still out back. Her screams made him come running. He saw Elizabeth's little body washed up on the beach and then Shelley started after him, screaming, crying, and beating on him. That, plus his own grief maybe—something—overwhelmed his senses and he swung the maul around, taking her head clean off her body. He chopped up the bodies and buried them under the floorboards."

Karen had drawn her feet up beneath her body. Her buzz was totally gone, and she was aching to go check on Becky, but the story had her in a kind of spell, and she needed to hear the rest.

Robert continued, "That's when things got really bad. Over the next few months, two little girls went missing from around the township here. It was even smaller then, and it didn't take long for the folks to figure out who was responsible. They gathered a crowd, and started to come for him, but before they could, he blew his head off with a shotgun. They found the missing girls buried under the floorboards, along with his wife and daughter."

"Jesus Christ, Robert," said Karen. "Why didn't they just tear it down?"

Robert crushed out his cigarette and lit another, "They can't. It belongs to a distant cousin of Shelley's. Guy's got more money than sense, but won't let anybody touch the place."

She shook her head in disbelief, "But that doesn't explain why it still seems so... ominous."

Her uncle nodded, eyes squinting against the smoke, "Here's the last part: Since Alvin McLaren died, four more little girls in the last twenty years have gone missing in this area. They've searched everywhere, but no sign was ever found. People just started suspecting the cabin had something to do with it. They said old Alvin gave up searching for girls to steal, and just waits there in his cabin like a spider, waiting for them to wander in."

He stood to leave, "And that's it. So—keep Becky away from that place, huh? We'll see you for breakfast tomorrow, okay?"

Karen was crying. "I'm going to go check on her. Goodnight Robert."

He went to her and gave her a hug. It felt so much like her dad that she cried even harder, missing him.

"Listen, Karen," he said. "I didn't tell you that to upset you, but I did want to scare you a bit. Scared is safe. Okay?"

She nodded, sniffing, and replied, "Okay."

The next morning, Becky was in a foul mood. She was normally a light sleeper and the storm had kept her up all night. She was fighting with Karen about everything.

After the ordeal that was breakfast, mother and daughter went for a walk on the beach. They'd only been walking five minutes when the pre-schooler tore off towards the brown cabin.

"I want to see the no-windows house!" She yelled back.

"Becky! Get back here!" Karen chased her. To her horror, as they approached, she saw the howling wind the night before had blown the door ajar, and Becky wasn't slowing down. The girl reached the threshold and ducked neatly under the piece of plywood that had been nailed across the doorway. As Karen caught up, the door banged shut. She could hear Becky on the other side, giggling madly.

"Becky!" Karen screamed, and heard the panic in her voice.

A long, silent moment passed. Then a piercing scream came through the door.

Karen shoved the door as hard as she could. It swung in easily and she ducked under the plywood. Becky was standing in the corner of a kitchen.

"Spider!" Becky pointed to the counter. The door slammed closed behind Karen, making them both jump. Near the rusted-out sink, there was a kitten sized daddy long-legs picking its way around several small animal skeletons that still had bits of mummified meat clinging to the bones. Karen took a deep breath, despite the oppressive heat and tickling dust.

"It's not a biting spider, Becky," said Karen, keeping calm—barely.

Becky was in front of one of the bedrooms now. Behind her, the room was dark—too dark. There should have been some light filtering in from the rotten roof, or around the boards on the windows. Instead, the shadows were total, and they were moving, extending themselves beyond the room, heading right for…

"Becky!" Karen screamed, "Get away from that room right now!"

Becky scowled at her mommy's tone. "No!" she shouted back, stomping her little pink-booted foot. The floorboard shook; all the floorboards shook in here. Karen ran at her daughter, scooping her up under one arm and bringing her to the door. It refused to open. She pulled the knob as hard as she could. It came away in her hands. They were trapped, and the shadows were moving outside the bedroom now. Karen darted into the other bedroom, which did have some light trickling in. Her sandaled feet crunched on something. The window in here had been smashed. She looked desperately around the room for something, some way to get out.

Something in the kitchen was laughing now. The sound hurt her mind. Of their own volition, the floorboards in here started rattling, trying to lift, trying to show her… something. Images of small lost faces flashed in Karen's head; delicate pale blue hands beckoned to her. Karen stood, helpless as the phantoms begged her to help, to stay.

Becky began to cry. The sound brought Karen back. Desperate now, she slammed the door against the darkness and saw a sledgehammer leaning against the corner. It had an ugly maroon stain along its handle. The blade was dull and coated with a mixture of rust and that same awful dark red.

Karen hefted the hammer and said, "Becky, back up, honey. I'm going to get us out." She swung it heavily at the board over the window. It gave a little with a shriek of rusting nails. The bedroom door started shaking in its frame. Karen swung again, and the board moved again. Fingers of shadow were creeping under the door now. Becky was screaming now. Karen swung the hammer one more time, and the bottom of the board was free. She grabbed Becky and lowered her out the gap, watching for rusted nails. The door swung open; there was nothing but blackness there. She dove at the gap and rolled out the window. Every nail she'd carefully avoided with Becky tore into her, digging deep, and she was soon bleeding profusely. She looked up at the window from the ground, and saw the board swinging out. There was a heavy, scratching, chitinous sound coming from within. She scrambled to her feet and slammed her ravaged shoulder into the wood. The board slammed home, driving splinters deep into her flesh. Something squealed in her head, furious at being denied. Big grey spots bloomed at the edges of her vision. She took a deep breath, and another. The day was warm, and the air was clean.

Becky was standing there, sobbing heavily, "I don't like that house, Mommy."

Karen hugged her tight, "Me neither, honey. Shh. Shh. It's all done now. All done."

***

Inside the cabin, the dark thing hissed one last time and coiled back upon itself. Alvin had all the time there was to sleep, and dream and wait.

FUN IN THE SUN

Billy shovelled sand onto Jamie's shoulders. His back hurt, he'd been digging for hours. Jamie still snored blissfully in the midday sun. The drug had worked perfectly.

Billy smiled. Danny was going to love this. Big bad Jamie, up to his neck in sand—it was too funny… too perfect.

For some reason, whether it was because he was the smallest, or because he had the balls to talk back to them, he always got the worst of it from Jamie and his friends.

What had happened last week, though, had crossed a line. What had happened last week had changed the rules forever.

***

They'd been playing basketball; Jamie had set an illegal pick that bloodied Danny's nose. Danny had been livid, and when Mr. Johnson turned away, he threw the ball at Jamie's head, knocking the big kid to his knees. That had done it.

After school, they'd squared off at the baseball diamond, just Danny and Jamie. None of the other kids had stepped into the circle. This was how it had to be.

As expected, Jamie had Danny to the ground in seconds, and was wailing on him. Danny's face was already swelling up.

"Do you like that, punkass? Feel like whipping a ball at me now?" Jamie punctuated each sentence with another shot.

***

Jamie was covered up to his upper arms now, and still showing no signs of waking. *God, you're a dick*, thought Billy. He remembered how Danny had turned it around and smiled again.

***

Billy had finally seen enough and started forward. Surprisingly, Danny saw him moving, and waved at him to stay back. The next moment, his knee was embedded in Jamie's crotch, and the big boy flopped over on his side. Danny rolled over and punched Jamie once—hard, just below his throat. Jamie gasped for breath. Danny stood and aimed a kick at the other's head. Billy grabbed Danny by the shoulders, and his guts turned to water as he saw pure hatred in his friend's eyes. After a moment, Danny stopped struggling and let himself be led away.

Two days later, Jamie had had his revenge. Nobody could prove he was the one who'd cut the brakes on Danny's bike, but enough kids had seen him by the bike rack that it was a pretty safe bet.

On his way home that night, Danny had gone charging down the hill toward his house, flying at top speed on the bike when he saw the train crossing come down. Billy was coming out of Dalton's Variety store with a Coke in his hand. He saw Danny holding his speed, waiting for the last possible minute to slam on the brakes and skid to a halt.

Except the bike kept hurtling forward. Danny's face became a mask of terror as he tried to turn the bike away from the tracks. It jerked, and he rolled off—into the path of the oncoming train. He was up and, with a second more, would've been safe. But that was a second he didn't get. The train roared past, cutting Danny in two.

Billy had run to the tracks as quick as his legs would carry him. His friend lay gasping beside the crossing.

"Billy?" asked Danny, in a soft, rational voice, "Billy, can you get help? I think I'm hurt badly."

***

He'd gone, too. Billy kept shovelling; Jamie's body was only visible from the shoulders up now. Billy took a sip of water, remembered the help he'd found, and wondered how lucky he really was.

***

Billy had run to the nearest house and started thumping on the door. The door of the place opened up, and a woman, huge and dark, was standing there.

"What you doing there, child? Don' you know better than to disturb Mamzel Daisy?" asked the woman with a voice that was heavily accented and full of unspoken danger.

A chill cut through Billy's grief. He'd inadvertently knocked on the door of the crazy witch woman. No one, not even Jamie's crew, would have dared go near the house, even on a dare. And now he was standing at her door. Still—Danny, he had to think of Danny.

"Please Missus," he'd said, "My friend... hit by the train. He's dying. Please. Please help."

"Lord help us," she'd replied, "Let's go, we got to go to him."

"But... the ambulance," Billy tried to insist.

The woman had looked over her shoulder and snapped, "You want to save the boy? Let's go."

They'd gone, but in the time it had taken him to reach the house, Danny had stopped breathing.

***

"There," said Billy, patting down the sand. Only Jamie's head poked free now. Yeah, Danny was going to appreciate this. Thanks to Mamzel Daisy, he'd get the chance.

***

"Oh, you poor child." The woman had gone to her knees and was cradling Danny. The strange intimacy of the moment made Billy avert his eyes, and he saw the bike—and the cleanly snipped brake cable.

"No," he'd said. "No, Jamie, you rotten bastard."

Mamzel looked up, "What is it?"

"I know who did this to him." Billy's voice had shaken with rage.

"Someone?" Mamzel's face had drawn down in a scowl. "Someone, took this child's life?"

"Yes. It was a boy at school. He cut the brakes; I'm sure of it."

Mamzel lowered Danny to the ground and looked at Billy. Her stare had been galvanizing.

"Listen, child." She'd said, "You want your friend back? You want this other boy to pay?"

Billy had replied without thinking; grief and rage had driven rational thought far from his mind, "Yes. Yes to both… but how?"

She'd nodded, "You leave that to Mamzel. But you give your word now—I'm puttin' this child's life in your hands. He's yours to care for. Will you?"

He'd agreed.

And with that, Mamzel had drawn a small package from her purse and started to chant.

***

"Wake up, jerk," said Billy, tapping Jamie on the head with his shovel.

Jamie's eyes snapped open, "What the fuck?" He flailed his head around before looking up again, "Let me go you little shit!"

Billy smiled, "Not yet. Someone wants to talk to you."

The bully started to say something back, but instead his jaw dropped open as he saw the shape pulling itself along the sand toward him.

"See?" asked Billy with a smile, "He's all right after all. I lied though, he doesn't say much anymore."

With eerie strength, Danny walked on his hands, closer and closer, trailing his sand-caked innards behind him. They could see the milky whites of his eyes now.

"I've been looking after him. Funny though, I couldn't figure out what he wanted to eat until now."

"Nnn. Nnnn." Jamie stuttered in terror, "No, man. Keep him away."

"Oh, come on. I had to give him a fighting chance. You can see he doesn't have a leg to stand on." Billy was laughing now.

This was going to be great.

SOMETHING DIFFERENT

Edna and Ralph were cozy in the back of his father's baby-blue Ford Fairlane. Slowly, the car began to rock. Their rhythm seemed to harmonize with the very sounds of nature all around them. Night birds courted among the lush canopy of trees, singing away the last faint rays of light. The golden-rimmed clouds parted, revealing the perfect orb of the full rising moon.

An unearthly howl filled the forest then, silencing all. The teenage lovers, lost in the perfect solipsism of young lust, heard nothing but their own haggard breath, moving faster and faster. It took the squeal of preternatural claws rending the metal flesh of the hardtop to jolt them from their…

***

"Carl, this isn't about werewolves, is it? They've been done to death. And teenagers? Next, they'll be meeting up with Laurel and Hardy. This is 3-D we're launching here. Three-god-damned-D. You're proposing we waste the single most exciting revolution in movie making on the same old shit that we've been turning out year after year?"

"People like werewolves, Mr. Anderson." Carl flushed purple, but had already moved the sheaf of papers to the bottom of a rather impressive stack.

"People liked Nixon at one point, Carl."

"Point taken, Mr. Anderson. Perhaps we could try something a *little* different."

"Yes, *different*. Now we're talking." The portly film exec leaned back in his padded chair. He lit another cigarette from the end of the one he was finishing and took a drag. "Go ahead, Carl. Wow me."

***

The new young master of the house arrived early in the day. The stately manor house had been a bequest of his recently departed uncle Chesterton. Putting aside the bizarrely hostile behaviour of the locals, including the rough young gent who'd shown him to the gate, he felt a kinship to the place. There was something in the air here that called to his blood.

It was only later that night, as he was making his way toward the lower chambers, that he got his first inkling of something amiss. All was silent, which was odd, as the house was draughty and should've been a haven for mice and rats.

The chamber at the bottom of the spiralling staircase was shut tight. Alvin put his shoulder to it, and grudgingly, it gave. Upon spying the large oblong box in the corner…

***

"Vampires, huh? That's different, Carl? You think any self-respecting teenager is going to strap blue and red glasses to his head to sit through… Listen, listen closely Carl—that sound you're hearing is Bela Lugosi spinning in his grave and the son-of-a-bitch isn't even dead yet. And again with the 'silent', we're making TALKIES here, Carl. Jesus."

Flustered, Carl drew in a deep breath and started muttering. It was so low it sounded like buzzing.

"What was that, Carl?" The exec was fuming. The meeting was a bust.

The scrawny writer pushed up coke-bottle glasses and cleared his throat. "I said I've got one more."

"Well, let's hear it."

***

The moon shone coldly with pale white light. The silence of the graveyard filled the air with ominous foreboding. In a far-off corner of the cemetery, the earth began to stir…

***

"I swear to God Carl, if it's fucking zombies, I'll garrotte you with that stupid purple necktie you're wearing. You're supposed to be a writing genius, Carl. You're a HACK!"

Carl was murmuring again, but Anderson took no notice, "Why on earth do I pay you? You're worthless—what's more... you're fired. Get out of my sight."

At this, Carl's face split in two, and released the monstrous flything that had been using him as a shell. Pincers like scimitars clicked in front of its mouth. Shaking off blood from its wings, it launched itself into the air, and sped toward Anderson. His last thought before his head was snipped from his body was, "Now *that's* what I was talking about."

FROSTED GLASS

Caroline held the glass ball up to the light again, as if this time it would reveal its secrets. Light penetrated and made it glow, but she just couldn't make out the thing inside. On the lower half, there was a crescent-shaped spot that looked like brown fluff, but it was like trying to look through a steamed-up shower door. With a sigh, Caroline lowered the sphere.

When she had purchased the glass globe earlier in the day, she had been looking for a "real" crystal ball to bring to the next girls' night out. Emmie, Jamie and Trina had all agreed that holding a séance sounded like a lot of fun and for Caroline, a crystal ball had seemed so much more original than showing up with a Wal-Mart Ouija board. This one had been high up on a shelf behind the counter at the occult shop, and the old woman at the till seemed loath to part with it, but had relented when Caroline offered double.

Deciding to take a more methodical approach, she removed her sweater and folded it on the dining room table, then placed the ball upon it. The swatch of brown was still there, pressed up against the glass. Caroline rotated the ball, and the brown rotated with it. She leaned in close to the surface and realized that it was definitely fur of some kind.

"What are you?" she asked and ran her fingers over the ball.

At the touch of her hand, the ball began to shimmer in the reflected light from the dining room chandelier. The outside of the ball became less hazy, and the fog seemed to retreat, forming a thick, swirling cloud within. The patch of fur resolved into the shape of a tiny creature. It stood on two legs, and looked faintly human, except for the thick brown hair that covered it. Caroline couldn't see more than that, as the curvature of the glass still obscured the finer details.

There was a tiny thump, and Caroline saw the thing had put its hands against the glass. I woke it up, thought Caroline. As she leaned in to take a closer look, it pressed its own face to the wall of its prison. Caroline got the impression of pale skin, hollow eyes, and a leering grin—it saw her. The hands disappeared from the glass, and the figure began to dance a bizarre, manic little jig.

Understanding only that she needed to see more clearly, Caroline picked up the ball. The thing reacted to her touch by increasing its pace, hopping and spinning like a top until it ended in a Vaudevillian *"Ta-da!"* flourish. Caroline smiled; wait until the girls saw *this*.

Without waiting for a response from her, the creature disappeared into the murk inside the glass. When it returned to view, Caroline was startled to see another figure had joined it. This one was quite different. It was paler, and seemed to be dressed up like a clown, from the riot of different colours that Caroline could make out. From its movements, though, it wasn't possessed of the same good humour as the furry one. Sitting at the dining room table, watching, Caroline could see the first little monster prodding the second, poking at it, trying to get it to move. Finally, the second little man, or whatever it was, began to dance. It was a pathetic imitation of the former performance. The thing's movements were slow and jerky, as if this was the last thing it wanted to do.

Caroline blinked and felt tears at the corners of her eyes. This poor thing was trapped and being forced to dance for her. She brought the ball up closer, cradling it in her arms, and tried to see more of the little dancer, who staggered slightly as the ball moved, but quickly regained its balance and stood still, watching her. It raised both its arms in a gesture of supplication, silently pleading.

The first, furry creature suddenly re-emerged from the murk behind the clown. It was an indistinct brown blob, but Caroline thought she could see something in its hands. It was a fuzzy thin line like a stick or…

There was a sickening thud, and the clown's head was thrown forward, smacking hard into the glass. It staggered to the side, leaving a white and red stain on the inside of the glass. The furry thing went berserk. It launched itself at the tiny clown, swinging the club again and again. Blood spattered the inside of the glass. The sounds were too loud. They seemed to be echoing inside Caroline's head. After what seemed like ages, the brown shape stopped swinging. It kicked the ruined clown once, and then stepped up on top of it. It gave another flourishing bow. *"Ta-da!"*

An instant later, the entire surface of the glass was filled up with the demonic black eye of the beast, staring directly at her. Seeing her. Studying her. Hating her. Caroline screamed and dropped the ball to the floor, where it broke with a dull crack.

The room began to fill with the white miasma from inside the globe. The ball was becoming completely clear, and it became harder and harder to breathe in the room. Caroline thought she could still see movement in the ball, but before she could be sure, the world swam in front of her, and went dark.

***

When Caroline awoke, the world was white. She was alone, resting on a cold, hard surface, surrounded by the same choking mist that had knocked her out.

As she tried to get up, she stumbled, and fell face-first back to the ground. Caroline recovered, and sat up, now noticing the blood red clown shoes on her feet.

Somewhere behind her, she heard movement, accompanied by breathy, chattering monkey sounds, and it was coming closer.

Hugging her knees to her chest, Caroline began to scream.

POSTAGE DUE, PANDORA

Katie thought the box was a joke at first.

The note on the plain brown craft paper read, in Stephen's carefully overwrought calligraphy,

"Thinking of you. S"

It had been waiting on the mail table in her front hallway when she'd arrived home. Looking at the package, she felt a tiny shiver at the nape of her neck. Putting it down to the air conditioning, after the humidity outside, she picked up the box. The first thing she noticed was how heavy it was, like it was full of rocks. She pulled her hair out of her eyes before the card got wet and unreadable. The skies had opened up about two blocks from home, and she'd had to run to avoid the worst of the downpour.

The gift was typical of her cousin Stephen. Currently, he was travelling in India, looking into a new group that was mixing ancient sitar raga, modern hip hop, and nu metal. At nineteen, he was the youngest-ever scout for Broken Needle Records. They'd been inseparable through six years of middle and high-school and the distance had strained their bond, but it had yet to break it. Before he left, though, Katie had given Stephen a hard time, accusing him of leaving his family and friends behind. She realized now that it had been a grossly unfair way to treat her closest companion, and worried about it constantly. The arrival of the package was a good sign—it had to be.

The postmark on the wrapping indicated he'd sent this from Mumbai. Katie peeled off the wrap to find a powder blue box, with gilded yellow scrollwork and long fabric tassels at the corners. *But powder blue?* Katie smiled. In the last three years at high school together, Stephen had defined goth for her, and she had gladly followed his lead, dressing exclusively in black for the remainder of their high-school years, earning them both the title of "the Trauma Twins." If Stephen was buying her something powder blue, then things had definitely begun to change.

She was starting up to her room when her mother called from the kitchen, shouted actually, to be heard over her "Crazy Eighties" CD, which she always put on when she was doing housework. "What was inside the package, honey?" she asked.

"It's a wooden box, Mom. From Stephen. I haven't opened it yet, but it looks pretty funny."

"Funny how?" There was a hint of ice in her tone. Donna liked Stephen but had never quite forgiven him for taking Katie to get her first tattoo when she was eighteen.

"Um, it just doesn't look like Stephen's taste, or mine, for that matter."

"Can I see it?"

"Not right now, Mom, 'kay?" Katie tried hard not to lose patience. She didn't really need to do the full-on rebellion thing with her Mom, but she'd ditched her cigarette about three blocks from home and had been chewing on strong mint gum ever since. The last thing she wanted right now was facetime with Mom. Smoking she wouldn't understand. She called down the hall, "I want to check it out first."

"Okay honey, dinner in half an hour, 'kay?" Katie heard the sound of running water, and the catchy synth of *I Ran* was turned up. She went upstairs before she had to listen to her mother singing along.

She was so focused on the package she could hardly look away, and stumbled on the last step, sending the box flying out of her hand. A previously unnoticed card shook loose of the wrapping and landed nearby.

She picked up the card, which was the same powder blue shade as the box, and had red Sanskrit on the top line, with English underneath.

"There is nothing in the box."

Underneath that, written quickly in Stephen's handwriting, which seemed oddly rushed and shaky,

"Yes, there is."

Intrigued, Katie picked up the box and the brown paper, went into her bedroom, and closed the door.

Sitting on the bed, Katie held the box in both hands, and began to examine it. The hasp was standard. She'd had a half dozen diaries and jewellery boxes growing up that operated the same way, with a tiny gold hook and eyelet.

She was about to unlock the lid when her eyes caught sight of the card again, with Stephen's hastily scrawled message. It was interesting that he'd been in such a rush to write this one, but then had taken care to sign the outside packaging with his usual careful calligraphy.

Katie shook the box. It seemed empty, just an ordinary jewellery box, probably with little compartments inside. She was lowering the box back to the bed when she felt something inside rolling around. It hadn't been there a second ago, or it most certainly would have made a clatter when she shook it. Still though, she tilted her wrist to the right, and the something inside shifted again.

Little hairs were standing up on the back of her arms now. Whatever was rolling around in there sounded alive. This was a ridiculous thought, she realized. It was probably a marble, or maybe some little piece of ornamentation that she'd broken loose with her shaking and would be kicking herself for ruining in a couple minutes' time. Nonetheless, the thought wouldn't go away.

Katie decided to set the box on her perfectly flat night table, and study it for a little while longer. She set her present down; its weight now seemed heavier than before, and warmer.

The sound came again. Rolling, rolling.

"This is stupid." Katie said aloud, trying to establish some sense of reason. It was probably some gag thing that Stephen picked up, full of magnets or something. It was like the rattlesnake eggs that her dad brought home one time. You got all worked up, she thought, and when you opened it up it was just a rubber band and a clothespin.

Katie thumbed the latch, forcing herself to laugh at her jitters. She lifted the lid by one of its golden tassels.

Free from the box, a small white marble flung itself into the air and landed squarely on Katie's lap. The split second before it spun around, she knew what it would be.

The eye looked at her, and she looked back. In its silver iris, Katie felt, rather than saw, intelligence and anger. It's not rattlesnake eggs, she thought.

Katie uttered a small grunt of disgust, and flung the marble across the room, where it happened to go through the door, into her bathroom. She hurried after it and slammed the door, hoping it wouldn't be able to roll underneath. Her heart was racing. She waited a few minutes to see if the eye would come back. It was silent, except for her mother's muffled singing coming up the stairs outside.

She went back to the bed and sat down. She picked up the box and lay back to study it. The inside was black velvet, much like her other jewellery boxes, but this stuff was darker than anything she'd ever seen before. It must have been an illusion, but she couldn't see the bottom of the box. She held it up to the light, and still the blackness persisted, and seemed to go on forever.

Katie's train of thought broke off suddenly, as she heard her door open, heard the knob twist, and the catch release. She heard the door swinging open. She looked up, and saw that, in fact, her door remained firmly shut. There was a soft thumping sound, like footsteps in the shaggy green carpet, and they seemed to be getting closer. Now she could hear breathing. It was the slow, heavy sighs of something very large. She heard a rough scratching as the something pushed its thick hide through her open door. (*It's closed,* her eyes insisted).

The breathing was louder now. She could hear her own breathing too, as it was now coming in short panicked hitches. (But there's nothing *there.*) An image formed in her mind of something that walked on two feet, made up of the bald and stretched pink skin of a recovering burn victim. Where this came from, she didn't know, but as soon as she thought it, she knew it was true. There was a monster in her room, and it was making its way toward her. (But the door is *closed*—the *door is closed*—there's *nothing there!*) Her mind was wailing now at the contradiction before her.

Thump. A huge and meaty foot hit the floor inside her room. *Thump.*

Katie screamed and bolted upright. The breathing stopped. The thumping stopped. The door was still closed. Her heart was pounding. No, stupid—your heart is thumping, get it? Katie closed the box and shook her head. This was all a little too weird for her. She'd have to have a long, serious talk with Stephen when he got back.

CLACK.

The bathroom door shuddered. Katie looked around and saw the eye, now wedged firmly under the door, and shaking the door violently, trying to get free. Its tiny black pupil was gone, and the silver iris stared at her, the stare of a dead thing.

Katie screamed at the bedroom door, "Mom? Mom! Help me!"

There was no reply from downstairs. The bathroom door was rattling on its hinges as the eye jerked and shuddered, working its way out of its temporary prison.

Then, nothing. Seconds passed. Katie could only hear the pounding of her heart in her ears. She looked at the door, and the eye was gone. Everything was still; she couldn't even hear the music from downstairs anymore.

"Mom? *Mom?*" Where was she? "Mom!" Katie felt six years old again and separated from her mother in a department store. She felt small, lost, and afraid.

There was no answer. She heard the doorknob start to turn again. "No!" she shouted. It would *not* happen again.

With a queer doubling of her vision, the room blurred in front of her. A moment later, the sensation passed, and everything suddenly seemed normal again.

Nothing. There was no such thing as a disembodied eye that moved and rolled on its own. It was ridiculous. Sudden movement caught her eye, and she jerked her head to see her own pale reflection staring back at her. Her own eyes looked red and, touching her cheek, she realized she'd been crying.

CLACK.

Katie jumped slightly at the sound and spun around to look at the bathroom door. Nothing there.

She decided she'd had enough. Time to go downstairs, help Mom finish dinner and forget all about this. Smoky clothes be damned.

She turned her door handle. It was locked. She jerked at the knob again and again. Behind her, the bathroom door began to shake again. The hinges were starting to rattle. Incredibly, the force was starting to shake them loose.

Suddenly, there was a new sound. It was a soft scraping at her feet. She looked down and saw a plain white envelope, with "Katie" scrawled hastily on it.

She tore it open and read:

Katie,

Your father and I have been quite unhappy for some time now, about seventeen years, give or take.

We've had long discussions about this, and we've decided that the best thing to do is just start over. We were never cut out to be parents. Hopefully we've faked it well enough that you won't end up on drugs or homeless, but in any case, it's time that we get on with our own lives.

We didn't want to leave you completely helpless, so here is some money to get you started on your new life without us.

Hope it's a good one.

Mom and Dad.

P.S. We sold the house. You have until tomorrow to get out.

P.P.S. There is nothing in the box.

Katie sat down hard as the walls spun around her. Everything was still, and she could hear the whispery scratch as the letter hit the floor and spilled out a handful of twenties. Her heart felt like a small hard stone throbbing painfully back and forth on overtaxed rubber bands. She was too shocked to cry. Her entire world had changed for the worse in the last half hour, and she found she simply didn't have a response. The door creaked open now, revealing empty halls. There were light spots on the paint where pictures had hung. Even the carpet was gone. She didn't need to leave the room to know that the rest of the house was just as empty.

Hadn't she just been speaking to her mother? Not twenty minutes ago, she'd left her mother singing and dancing in the kitchen. *You were preoccupied*, she thought, *you were dealing with imaginary eyes, and fake monsters*. The voice of her thoughts sounded distinctly petulant. The Cure could've played a special one-time show in your kitchen just now and you wouldn't have noticed because you were too busy having your little panic attack over what? A scary marble? You're pathetic.

Hearing her own thoughts attacking her was enough to start the tears flowing. She lowered her head and let the sobs come. She cried because she was scared. She cried because she wanted her mother. She cried for her broken life.

Spasms wracked her body, and she could feel the sting of her makeup running and snot dripping off her chin. After what seemed ages, the awful hitching in her chest slowed, and she wiped her face on her t-shirt, leaving a gummy whitish smear behind. She looked at the money lying on the floor and tried to think of what to do next.

CLACK.

The rolling sound came back. It was amplified now, and had a metallic echo. Katie's eyes went to the heating duct. It had found a way out of the bathroom after all. The cover was still in place, just next to the door. But would it hold?

There was a heavy sounding click, and the lights went out. She could barely see now by the dusky light coming through her rain-streaked bedroom window. All too soon, the bruised purple would fade to twilight blue, and she'd be practically blind. And trapped in an empty house with the eye, she thought, don't forget that. She moved backward, keeping her focus on where she thought she remembered the duct to be.

The rolling came again. The eye was ricocheting off the walls of the ductwork, like a marble in her old mousetrap game. It sounded like it was right behind the bedroom grate now.

Katie finally understood. This wasn't happening. This was some kind of hallucination. She must have hit her head when she tripped up the stairs. For all she knew, she was still lying there at the top of the stairs with a possible concussion.

It was the only thing that made sense. There was no other way so many things could be happening just to her, and so close together. No way at all.

There was a squeal of metal, then… more rolling. Rolling. Stop. She looked down, and there was the eye.

She laughed. "You're not real. Get lost."

The eye spun around once and fixed its glare on her again. Faintly, she could hear the muffled thumping footsteps making their way down the hallway again.

Sudden red rage gripped Katie, and she grabbed the eye—meaning to throw it as she had before. This time, though, her arm convulsed as energy coursed into her from the eye. She was frozen in place, staring into its dead silver iris. She heard the mutant-thing in the hall bellow. It was a choked, watery sound, like it was screaming through a mouthful of meat. She was certain then that this eye belonged to that beast.

Katie was afraid. She felt terror pumping into her like liquid. It hurt to breathe, her heart hurt to pump. Her pants turned dark as, with a noiseless rush, her bladder emptied its contents.

"Why are you doing this to me?" She screamed in her head, but all that came out of her mouth was a tortured squeak. Somehow, though, the eye heard her, and increased the flow of energy.

As suddenly as it had begun, the awful pulsing stopped, and Katie collapsed onto her knees and the eye rolled out of her hands and across the floor. She took several deep breaths, watching the eye now, wary of further harm.

The thumping steps started again. Her mind clawed for purchase. Because asking "why" had worked out so badly, she found herself replaying the list she'd first heard in Mr. Allen's Grade 11 English class. "Everything you want to know about the world, kids, you can find out with one of these six questions—'Who, what, where, when, why and how.' If you run out of things to say, ask one of these questions." Mr. Allen had been a total jackass that year, passing her with a lowly sixty-one, but that little nugget of wisdom had stayed with her.

So, the questions "why" was out. Maybe she could get a grip on things if she could just stop for a second and for chrissakes think!

Thump. She felt her anger return, and threaten to cloud her judgement again. No. Just ignore it for a second and think. Her brain looped the loop and the sequence started again.

Who? Me, just me.

Where? My house, but it's not really my house anymore. Everything's gone freaky.

THUMP

What? No way. Too big, too weird. I'll go even crazier.

When?

The eye spun around then and fixed her with the dead silver of its gaze again. It hopped up about an inch and clacked against the wood floor as it came back down.

When? There was something there. When did all this madness start? Something in her mind clicked as loud as the eye had. When she'd opened the box. *The box.*

There is nothing in the box.

Yes, there is.

Everything had begun with the box.

Thump. Katie could hear the creature now, scraping along the hallway. It was slowed by the width of the hallway, but it would be on her soon. She realized something had finally gone her way.

"There is nothing in the box." Repeating this over and over, Katie felt that if she could only prove this to herself all this would be over.

Picking up the robin's egg blue box, she lifted the lid once more. This time it fought. Though she had wedged her fingers under and was pulling with all her strength, there was a brief moment when she feared it would simply snap shut and sever the joints at the knuckle. There'd be something in the box then, she thought with a shudder and kept pulling. Finally, it popped open without warning. It just seemed to give up. The inside of the box had changed as well. Gone was the deep black velvet. The inside of the box now seemed to be made up of darkness itself. "Nothing," she said aloud, "That's what I'm looking at. There is nothing in the box."

Still, her plan was all she had, and from the sound of destruction now coming from downstairs, the thing was forcing its way around to resume the chase. Underneath that, a smaller, sharper sound. The click, click, click of something small bouncing on hardwood. Glancing to her left, the eye was staring back at her.

Oh, right. That thing, she thought, and on the tails of that came motivation, Alright Katie, quit thinking about it and just do it.

Katie jammed her hand down into the box, and it immediately felt all wrong. The black insides of the box enveloped her hand, sucking it in like a muscular throat, swallowing her down. No. Her inner-voice broke in fiercely, like a slap in the face. It's playing its games again. If you let it, it'll kill you. Just break through it. You have to take control, or it's over. The blackness felt moist, and it was moving now, gulping. Katie gritted her teeth and spread her fingers open wide. Her nails, long and coated with black polish, raked against the insides of the box. The shape of the box was just barely discernible beyond the membrane. The blackness reacted immediately, spasming against her. Katie felt something sharp, like teeth. Splinters, it's just splinters. Go on. The darkness bit. She felt the flesh on the back of her hand give way and blood start to flow. With a small grunt of pain, Katie raked her hands down the sides, feeling all the while for the shape of the wood. Under the circumstances, she wasn't surprised to find that she was now up to her elbow in a box that had fit in her palm when she'd first opened the package. The blackness pulsed again. More splinter teeth dug in, clawing their way through her palm now.

Nightmare images flooded Katie's mind and became real all around her room. Dead animals twitched in the corner. A shadowy figure was doing something horrific to another form bound against the wall. They insisted themselves upon her, demanding she look.

Katie pushed down harder into the box, and dug deeper with her fingers, scoring the wood now. The pressure threatening to bend her fingernails back, or rip them off completely. The blackness was up to her shoulder now, and she had to get her head closer to the box to reach further in. The box was breathing. It gave short quick gasps, like the shallow panting of a wounded animal. It was hurt.

With renewed strength, Katie thrust deeper, clawing the insides of the box, and finally, she was rewarded, finding the outline of something hard and round, a ring—it seemed—just under the flesh. Seizing it with all her strength, Katie pulled. The membrane jerked and pulled at her hands, the splinters dug deeper. The door crashed in and remained intact, releasing the invisible shambler to make its short final trip to ravage her.

She wrenched with her hand again and felt the membrane tear slightly. Emboldened, she pulled harder.

A sharp *CLACK* made her jerk her head up. The eye was balanced on the lid of the box, and stared at her with impotent rage. Something in her bicep strained and popped. She let out a single cry of pain and tugged again. With a final jerk, the ring came free of the box. Immediately, the shambler's thumping footsteps stopped. In front of her, the eye evaporated in a puff of robin's egg blue smoke. She looked at the ring. It was a small thing made of tarnished copper. Attached was a metal and plastic luggage tag. Inside the tag was stuffed a small, folded slip of paper:

Katie,

    I hope you're reading this. If you are—I'm so sorry.
    Once you open the box, it doesn't stop until you give it away. I tried once to warn you not to open it, but then it came back to me. I tried again with just a small hint, and obviously, it worked.
    I love you, Kates. And I'm proud of you for winning.
    Be well, and for god's sake don't start buying top 40 just because I'm not around.

Stephen.

Katie read the note again, and then a third time, hating Stephen one moment, and missing him terribly the next. She lamented that this had come to her, and despaired that she would be passing misery onto someone else.

When she lifted her eyes from the paper, she wasn't surprised to see her room had returned, and that she could hear her Mom, still singing downstairs.

One week later, Katie sat down at her desk. She had Shannon's yearbook message to her open on the desk, the one which proclaimed them "BFFs." The school year after she'd signed this missive, Stephen had been gone for six months, and Shannon had thrown herself at Mark Norman, the very day after Katie had confessed her secret crush.

Taking the pretty red and yellow gift tag, Katie signed it,

Dear Shannon,

   Thinking of you.

Love, Katie.

P.S. There is nothing in the box

EAT ME

Above, perched in the carnelian cap of its toadstool, the immense blue caterpillar leaned out into space.

Alice was very small, and the taste of mushroom lingered at the back of her throat.

"Really," it said, voice harrumphing, "It is very difficult to converse when you keep *changing* so." Smoke billowed down from its nostrils and rolled across the ground like fog.

Alice breathed deeply and coughed. She understood everything at last. When you got all the way to the end of curiouser things started making sense again.

She grinned up at the caterpillar.

"Piss off, you cranky old twat. You're killing my buzz."

Lying in the rich smelling grass, Alice began to fade, and the last thing to go was her smile.

ON-Y DANCER

Lars's friends thought he was foolish to want to visit the ruins of the Moulin Rouge. The serving girl at the inn, a clumsy but well-endowed brunette named Chantelle, had practically warned him against it.

"There is nothing there, monsieur. It has not even been touched since the fire. I think it is dangerous to go there."

What she couldn't know was that was the reason Lars wanted to see the place. It was the unasked question that drove him—why? Why had this landmark been left in ruin? In Paris—setting aside the cabaret's history—the property alone was worth a fortune. Yet, as Lars approached, the blackened brick façade, he found Chantelle's words to be the truth—there was no sign of anything or anyone having touched the building since the time of the conflagration.

He found the front doors sealed up with rough, carefully hammered planks. A yellowing notice was pasted to these, declaring the property "A vendu." It was enough to answer one question for him, at least. The Moulin had not lain empty for lack of trying.

Around the side, Lars found that the boards over the stage door were loose. He pried several of these all the way off, wincing as the rusted nails came free from the swollen wood with squeals of protest, and checking frequently over his shoulder for passing gendarmes. The door behind the boards was so charred it broke free of the jamb with minimal pushing.

Inside, the air was cool, but still smelled of ash and something else beneath—an unpleasant greasiness that Lars couldn't identify.

As he made his way into the grand hall, his breath caught in his throat. The enormous room was a disaster of fallen beams and shattered chandeliers, but it was simple for Lars, who had obsessed over this monument to pleasure, to close his eyes and fill the room from the details in his memory. When he looked again, he could picture the dozens of wealthy, hot-blooded patrons, and the enticing can-can girls that tempted them moving about the place. The very wood of the place sang with the ecstasy of evenings devoted solely to the teasing promises of young, firm flesh.

Suddenly, from behind the stage, Lars heard a noise. Tinkling laughter reverberated through the dead space like crystal wind chimes. He sprinted back the way he'd come, across a ruined dance floor and up several black, broken steps that lead to the dressing rooms.

When he reached the hallway he'd entered, he stopped at a singed, mouldy red velvet drape on his left. On his way in, he'd peeked inside, only to see a long, empty, burned out room with a few sticks that looked like the remains of furniture.

Now the room was filled with warmth and light from dozens of candles in iron candelabra. Dressing mirrors along one side reflected the bright amber light and made it sparkle. A moment ago, everything had been black, grey and descending into ashes. Now, all was colour. The walls screamed with brilliant yellow paint, and the floor had been restored to a deep and lustrous walnut hue.

A flicker of movement caught his eye, and when he turned his head, he gasped. Where, just moments before, he'd been alone in the room, there were now seven young women standing near the wall, talking and giggling.

There was too much to look at. The women had been caught, it seemed, amid preparations for a show, and were only partially clothed. Swells of breasts and buttocks pressed and strained against ornate, yet delicate, bustiers and garters. It overwhelmed Lars' senses. He could smell perfume and the faint odour of burnt hashish. There was nowhere to look that was not beautiful.

"Bonsoir, monsieur," breathed a short blonde ghost to his left. "Voulez-vous couchez avec nous?" She was barely dressed in a white corset with green ruffles of lace that drew his eyes to her delectable curves. His body throbbed for the courtesan phantoms.

There was no questioning the intent. He was wanted here. He was wanted.

"Yes... oui. *Oui!*" Lars stammered, determined to give in to the experience. He would taste and savour the pent-up sexual energies of a century.

"Ah, monsieur, *c'est bien*." said another, peeking over the top of an ostrich feather fan.

She lowered it, and Lars saw that only her eyes had been untouched by the blaze. His rising excitement was instantly quenched with cold and certain dread. The scents in the room changed from perfume to rot, from incense to charcoal. As the women surrounded him, their façade of flesh melted away, revealing their charred and ruined true forms beneath.

Somewhere, music started playing.

STORY NOTES

Hi there.

If you've gotten this far—you can stop reading and do so with my great thanks for having shared these stories of mine. The notes I've included below are not in the least bit necessary for your enjoyment of the preceding tales.

Why include them, then? The most honest answer is the simplest—when I read a collection of short stories, I like reading the notes section at the end as well.

So, if you're like me, then here we go!

Coming Home started at the ending.

One night, when I was still living alone, I was in that weird state between awake and dreaming. I'd just gone to bed and suddenly, I sensed a presence in the bed with me. I even thought I heard a voice saying, "welcome back." There was nothing to see, but the sensation was creepy as hell, and stayed with me. The rest of the plot owes itself to my "noir" stories. Mr. Dallas is a crime boss that pops in a lot of my stories. (He's in here twice.)

Sex and Beer started as a 100 word drabble for Lily Childs' "Friday Prediction Challenge". I can't remember the three prompt words anymore, but I really liked the story—enough that I expanded it for a guest writer spot at David Barber's "Flash Fiction Offensive." The ending was tremendously fun to write. I could've kept twisting for another three pages.

Scratch was another "Friday Prediction." There's a streak in my writing that doesn't pop up often, but when it does, it's mean. When I wrote this, I wanted to push the discomfort as far as possible. I'd write more about this, but I'm incredibly itchy right now.

Bones of Contention is one of three stories that appeared in the *Unquiet Earth* anthology, from Static Movement. This one grew from that first question about the skeletons. When I'm writing zombie stories, I'm way more interested in the relationships of the survivors than the actual undead killing part. In the case of the Zombie Apocalypse, we need to be prepared for the very real possibility that annoying people will survive too.

The Doll Maker and the Rat was my "Bonus Story" for the first ever "Eight Days of Madness" event on my blog. The key here, aside from the theme of "madness", was to see what happened if I put an extreme twist at the *beginning* of the story, and then had to make it work.

Devil's Night is what happens when I try to write a straight up "haunted house" story. It's new for this book. The house itself is an amalgam of several big creepy houses that we used to skip over while trick-or-treating when I was a kid.

Pick Your Own Pumpkin features two of my favourite characters to write, Milton and Blackwood who are named (obviously) for John Milton and Algernon Blackwood. They are regular detectives that seem to always end up on the "weird" cases. I'm planning to give these fellows a larger project to stretch out in the future. The genesis of this particular plot? The wall o' pumpkins, and plenty of visits to the tourist farm.

Newspaper Hat is another "Prediction" entry. This character came out full formed, wearing his hat, and he started to speak.

Kittens for Sale was the first story I "sold" to an online publisher, Microhorror.com to be exact. It's now been published on two online Zines and two anthologies. I'm still haunted by the image at the end, which is why this piece is a personal favourite.

The Moustache is one of the only "made to order" stories I've ever written. I wrote this as a "thank-you" to everyone who supported my fundraising efforts last "Movember". It took a while to get started with the prompt "a story about a moustache" but once it started coming—it didn't want to end!

The Sins of the Past is the other story in this book that features Mr. Dallas and his go-to guy, Gerard. If I ever want to write another story with these guys, I suppose it will have to be in the past. Also, I like werewolves.

The Choir of Pulcinello started life as a fifteen-page poem that I wrote for a Historical Horror anthology. Given the scathing rejection I got, I gained a significant respect for what poets do with words, and how much of a poet I am not. It was reworked for Microhorror.com's Halloween contest, also featuring Horror through History as a theme, and my weird and gruesome puppeteer finally found a home.

Game Night was the first "long" piece I placed, in an edition of Oddville Press. I write a lot about poker, and yet I almost never play. I have no idea why that is. (And "ghost farts" made me laugh when I wrote it.)

Adaptation was written based on a photo prompt—specifically a large ruby in a bird's nest. It hatched from there.

Tempting Morsels is based on my grandmother's butterscotch pie.

Turn Around came about when I thought about that instinctive knowledge that all people seem to have when someone is watching them—even if it's completely quiet. What *is* that?

Fear Combined was written with the *Howl* anthology in mind. There were two problems, though—the first was that I missed the cut-off and the second was that I have a problem staying inside the lines with "classic" genre stories. Truthfully, though—it's not a problem, I just don't care to. The main creation is inspired by some of the monsters in the Final Fantasy series of video games but adding the human element to the Chimera myth was where this story really started to take off.

Mopping Up is the most "zombie" of the zombie stories in here. I'm intrigued by the idea of "the zombie problem" being more or less over, and civilization trying to start itself up again. That was the beginning of this, and then I got a little silly with the animals. Come on, zombie mice?

A Fairy Tale came about because, as a dad, I'm now reading a lot of fairy tales. This story is wish fulfilment for all those times that "happily ever after" doesn't quite pay for all the suffering that's come before.

Treasures of the Deep was written for *The New Flesh*. Their contest theme was "Why I keep my eye in a pickle jar." The trouble was that I got so carried away writing the mermaid story I'd always wanted to pen, that I almost forgot to squeeze the prompt in there!

Freedom Within Reach was a Microhorror Halloween contest story. The theme was "space", and I immediately started thinking about those last few inches between sane and insane.

The cabin in **The Cabin Sleeps** is a real place. Growing up, my family had a cottage on a bay that fed into Lake Superior. This brown, beaten down cottage had always been boarded up as long as we'd been there, and it was the very first "haunted house" that I've ever been in. It was incredibly creepy to see all the random bits of stuff that had been abandoned years and years ago.

Fun in the Sun combined a few of the common threads that crop up in my stories—zombies and adolescents. That I go back to the latter so often tells me I'm still very much an adolescent myself, in the story-telling department as well. I can only try to put an adult's sense of how to tell the stories my inner juvenile delinquent insists on sharing. The other thing to take from this? Bullying sucks.

Something Different is really just me asking what a lot of people ask when our pop culture record starts skipping and repeating the same damned thing over and over and over. You want zombies? Here's *all the zombies*.

I wrote **Frosted Glass** for Erin Cole. More correctly, I wrote it for her *13 Days of Horror* event. It's the first time I wrote a story with only my desired effect and tone to go on. The plot itself is rooted in my love of TV shows like The Twilight Zone, Amazing Stories!, and Tales from the Crypt.

Postage Due Pandora had a rough life as a story. I started it out as a group exercise for a Toronto writer's group I was attending at the time. I wanted to try my hand at an Edgar Allen Poe type plot. (Specifically, I had the *'Imp in the Bottle'* in mind as inspiration when I started out.) I couldn't find a home for it, and ultimately released it as a serial on my own site. The invisible monster at the door is another weird "audio" dream that I had one time. Freaked me right out.

Eat Me was me wanting to see Jefferson Airplane's Alice actually going to Wonderland. Apparently, she's still British, though.

On-y Dancer was a "Friday Prediction," and came from specific prompt words. Once I started, the central image that pulled it all together was of Lars being simultaneously horrified and turned on. If I ever write anything longer about the Moulin Rouge, I will have to do more than Wikipedia research, however, so apologies to those of you who've been.

ACKNOWLEDGEMENTS

Writing is a pretty solitary affair. You sit, you write, and you sort of get on with it. When a story is complete though, it becomes apparent that *nothing* is going to happen to that story without some help.

I've had a lot of help to get here.

First, I've got the best wife in the world. Aimee supports me in my quest to get published, and she lets me get away with absolutely *nothing* when she's helping me edit.

My parents got me reading early and encouraged me to pick up a pencil and write my own stories back when I was still in the single digits. For that I'll always be grateful.

The stories in this book owe their lives to a group of superheroes masquerading as Online Magazine and Small Press editors, so huge thanks go to: Nathan Rosen, Lori Titus, Brian Barnett and William Pauley III, Col Bury and Matt Hilton, Chris Bartholemew, Jessy Marie Roberts, Michael C. Pennington, David Barber and the inimitable Lily Childs.

Finally, to my writing friends around the globe: Your support and your comments have made a huge difference in my writing and my life. There are too many to list everyone, but I need to give special mention to Jodi, Angel, Becky and Laurita—thanks for everything.

ABOUT THE AUTHOR

Chris Allinotte lives in Winnipeg with his wife, children, and one rambunctious black and white dog.

In 2008, his story "The Dirt on Ronnie Wilkins" won first place in the Toronto Star Short Story Contest. As a result of winning the contest, Chris got to attend the prestigious George Brown College Writer's course, where he studied for eight months with author Tim Wynne Jones.

Chris is the creator and editor of the *Days of Madness* anthologies. His work appears in the *Parallel Prairies* anthology, and he is a frequent contributor to *The NoSleep Podcast*.

Printed in Dunstable, United Kingdom

65271653R00092